A Fine Couple

THE GERMAN LIST

Gert Loschütz

A Fine Couple

Translated by Simon Pare

Seagull
BOOKS

LONDON CALCUTTA NEW YORK

This publication has been supported by
a grant from the Goethe-Institut India.

Seagull Books, 2022

Originally published in German as
Ein schönes Paar by Gert Loschütz

Copyright © 2018, Schöffling & Co. Verlagsbuchhandlung GmbH,
Frankfurt am Main

First published in English translation by Seagull Books, 2022
English translation © Simon Pare, 2022

ISBN 978 1 80309 066 5

British Library Cataloguing-in-Publication Data
A catalogue record for this book is available from the British Library

Typeset by Seagull Books, Calcutta, India
Printed and bound in the USA by Integrated Books International

Lovers, if Angels could understand them, might utter
strange things in the midnight air. For it seems that everything's
trying to hide us. Look, the trees exist; the houses
we live in still stand where they were. We only
pass everything by like a transposition of air.

Rainer Maria Rilke, *Duino Elegies*
(J.B. Leishman and Stephen Spender trans)

1

A stereoscope is a device for viewing pairs of stereo images taken with a stereo camera. The slight lateral discrepancy produces an impression of spatial depth: you think the person is actually in front of you. Peer through the stereoscope, and you are alone with him or her. You have to press your eyes tight to the eyepieces, and this blocks out all other visual impressions, enabling you to fully focus on the subject's features.

I could imagine that lovers forced to live apart were delighted by this invention—for a time, at least, until this nonphysical proximity drove them mad. The others who invested hope in this technology were criminologists. It allowed them to study the culprit's face. Might it not be possible to trace the horrific act, the puzzle posed by the crime, by reading the perpetrator's face, like a hunter studying the hoof prints of a wild beast? Maybe this landscape of hillocks and hollows, which, unlike traditional photographs, invited the finger to trace it, would provide the elusive explanation?

Lovers and criminologists, then. And, ultimately, both were disappointed didn't.

Wüstenhagen, the dealer in whose shop I sometimes nosed around for old cameras, rang me in the morning and said, 'I've got a stereo camera made in 1919. Interested?' I was, yes. But he hummed and hawed when I enquired about the price. He would first have to ask the man who had commissioned him to sell the thing, he said.

'Go ahead,' I said and after hanging up it occurred to me that it was the year of his birth. 1919 was the year of my father's birth.

I went up to my office in the attic, and Wüstenhagen rang back as I was coming down again that evening.

'I've got the price,' he said, but his quote was so ridiculously high that I declined.

Two calls from Wüstenhagen. And during the night a call from Frau Roth, my father's housekeeper.

It was about half past one. The phone rang shrilly. I got out of bed, went into the hallway, picked up the receiver and heard sobbing, followed by a few words I couldn't understand, though I recognized the voice.

'Frau Roth?' I asked.

'Yes,' she replied and then told me that he had died. She had gone back to his flat that evening and found him dead in his armchair. The TV was on. He was sitting there as if he were still alive, but he was dead.

She spoke haltingly, her sentences interspersed with repetitions and pauses. She said she'd been with him in the afternoon and had dropped by again later to say she wouldn't be able to come the following week. She'd forgotten to tell him that afternoon. She had rung him but he hadn't answered the phone, which is why she had set off again up the hill; or rather, her husband had driven her there. She had rung the bell and, as he didn't open the door, she'd thought he wasn't in and used her key—she had a key, of course. She had unlocked the door and gone into the house to write him a note and put it on the kitchen table.

And there was something else she said whose significance became clear to me only later, and which she only mentioned because she'd hurt herself.

Stepping inside and unable to find the light switch, she had called his name and, taking a few steps along the hallway, bumped into an obstacle in the darkness: the ladder. The trapdoor leading up to the attic was unlatched, the ladder extended. Frau Roth had worked for him for 16 years since his retirement, but she had never seen this before. She never went up into the attic and was therefore unprepared for this.

She found him at ten, and the doctor arrived at half past ten and confirmed his death. She knew then that he was dead, but it took her another three hours to find the courage to dial my number.

Frau Roth was a short, squat woman with a broad face and round, slightly bulgy eyes. She wore her hair in a low plaited bun. On Friday evenings she and her husband could be seen making their way to the yellow brick building in the court gardens where the Free Church held its services. When they re-emerged their faces shone with a peculiar glow, the reflection of the strict, self-assured justice so typical of the region, but this did not diminish the affection they felt for my father. He might have been a godforsaken sinner, but his simple lifestyle reconciled them to him.

In one photo I took of them they are standing side by side, shoulder to shoulder, staring at the camera with their round eyes while my father, whom I was actually trying to photograph, sneaked out of the shot. The two of them at the front, he a silhouette behind the glass door. He didn't like being photographed or, rather, let's say, he didn't like the fuss around it, the whole palaver.

September it was. Frau Roth called in September.

I'd only seen the young man who rang up a month later three or four times, and I don't think we had ever exchanged more than a couple of words, hello, goodbye, and yet as soon as I heard his voice I knew who he was.

He was doing his community service in the home where my mother had spent her final years. We would sometimes bump into him when she accompanied me down the noisy staircase to the front door. He was usually wearing sandals and an ankle-length caftan made of a heavy fabric with a braid border. That wasn't the main thing I noticed about him, though; it was the strange way he looked at my mother. Whenever he caught sight of her, his eyes would take on a rapturous gleam. A sign of his reverence for an elderly lady? Maybe. He caressed her with his gaze (there's no other way of putting it) whereas he would stare up at me with something approaching rage, as if about to headbutt me in the chest. There was no question that he saw me as an intruder, a messenger from the world in which she used to belong.

This young man rang me a month after her death and yelled the news into my ear: 'She's dead, do you hear? Dead.' A second later, I heard the voice of the nurse who had grabbed the receiver from his hand: 'I do apologize, Herr Karst.'

This is what happened. The nurses had got used to her barricading her door by wedging the back of a chair under the handle, something they regarded as one of her many foibles; but when the handle still wouldn't move the next morning, the nurse who had come on duty at six sent the young man, who happened to be coming along the corridor, to fetch the caretaker, but instead of running the errand he charged the door and forced it open. Entering the room, they found her on the bed, fully dressed, her eyes closed as if she was asleep. The young man knelt down beside the bed and laid his hand on her cheek.

I hadn't really considered it then, but piecing together the clues now, I realize that he must have known my number by heart. He didn't need to look it up and when the nurse ordered him to get up, he rushed to the phone and rang me.

My father had moved six times, always within Tautenburg or around Tautenburg, each time to a better flat, each more different from the last one they had lived in together, and he finally settled in the house above the town—a bungalow with a large garden sloping down towards the town.

In the evenings he would go from one room to the next, letting down the blinds, then out into the hallway to release the hatch, a white wooden trapdoor with a metal ring into which you inserted a hook screwed into the end of a wooden pole; he would pull out the stepladder and climb up into the attic, whose roof was so low that he had to walk around stooped.

There were three small windows in the pitched roof. One of them looked out towards the Battery, a rocky bluff in the forest from which troops had bombarded and set fire to the Middle Franconian town during the Seven Years' War (children learnt about this in local history lessons), the second towards White Rock, a path dotted with benches that attracted young couples who didn't know where else to go in the evenings; the third and last offered a view over fir trees to the town.

At the same time each day, my mother would push the chair against the door and wedge its back under the handle as a pre-caution to keep out the nurse who made her rounds between eleven and half past. My mother wasn't doing anything wrong; she just didn't want to be disturbed by this (to her mind) coarse woman who—worse still—rolled her 'r's in the local dialect my mother loathed. Afterwards, she would pull back the curtains, open the window and look out.

Every evening at a fixed time.

I knew that the home served breakfast at half past seven. Since my mother refused to go to the common room where the others ate their breakfast—those who were capable of going there, that is—the nurses brought her breakfast to her room. She would be up and dressed when they came. She would eat a slice of brown bread and drink two cups of coffee; she sent everything else back. The same thing every morning.

'But Frau Karst,' the nurse said when she fetched the tray, 'you really must eat something.'

We had set off at eight and it was now half past nine. I went into my father's living room, shut the door behind me and rang her. She had a phone—a privilege she hadn't requested but had nevertheless been granted. She needed the small table it had originally stood on for her sewing machine, so she had put it on the floor under the washbasin near the door.

She let it ring a few times before picking up, and I told her what had happened. This was followed by a momentary silence which suggested to me that she hadn't understood.

'Did you hear me?' I asked.

'Yes,' she said before addressing someone who was apparently in her room—'Wait a minute and I'll help you'—then speaking to me again in the same cheerful tone, 'You'll never believe this. She knocked the bucket over. The mop bucket.'

'Did you get what I said?' I repeated.

'I'm not deaf.'

After a brief chat we hung up. Aside from a short phone call the next day and the few words we exchanged at the cemetery, that was our last conversation because she died a few weeks later.

*

Yes, that's what happened. First him, then her. Him in September, her in October. She came to his funeral, just as he later came to hers. Sounds odd, but that's how it was. It was Mila who spotted her.

The night Frau Roth called, the door swung open and Mila appeared. Woken by the phone, she got up and came into my room; she leant against the doorjamb and listened with her head tilted until it was practically resting on her shoulder. She had arrived that afternoon from Berlin. She refused to use the subway and had therefore taken a taxi from Frankfurt central station out to Enkheim. After a short walk through the marshes, she had sat down at my computer to look for photos for the programme. She had meant to travel back the next day, but when she heard what had happened, she changed her plans and came to Tautenburg with me.

She sent her selection of pictures to the theatre the next morning, before breakfast. An hour later—we were standing in the hallway, about to leave—her mobile rang. She gave no sign of retreating into one of the rooms and sat down on a chair instead, so I overheard her conversation. It was Annette, her assistant, and I gathered from the way they spoke, from Mila's trouble convincing the other woman that it was truly a bereavement that had delayed her return, and from the powers of persuasion she had to deploy to prevent the woman from joining her in Frankfurt (either from a longing to be with Mila or to check she was telling the truth) that the caller wasn't only her assistant but her lover too.

Mila was in her mid-fifties, but in the subdued light in the corridor she looked the way she had when we met almost 30 years before, except that her hair had taken on the same copper hue as all former brunettes of her age. Go out for dinner with her and you could be sure that, sooner or later, everyone, men and women, would stare, although it was often the women who drew the men's attention to her. One possible reason was that hers was a quiet kind of beauty; there was nothing showy about her, nothing that might come across as overbearing unless, that is, someone found the regularity of her features or the restraint of her clothes and demeanour overbearing. (Which it presumably was, although this didn't alter her impact.) Sometimes, it seemed to me that her simple presence had an educational effect. She spoke quietly and so everyone else lowered their voices. She made no fuss about her work or herself, so chronic smart-arses and show-offs controlled themselves around her. She didn't drink alcohol or hardly any (maybe two watered-down glasses of wine over the course of an evening), so the boozers at her table would forego a couple of their customary drinks. The incredible thing, though, was that her soothing influence lingered after her departure. Even afterwards, the tone would remain measured; the bigmouths lowered their gaze and the thirsty practised moderation, responding to waiters' questioning glances with a shake of their heads.

*

Herta had received the news of his death with the same indifference she showed for everything I told her about him, and so I didn't know if it had actually got through to her. Maybe, I thought, it had snagged in the lengths of fabric she liked to drape around herself. The funeral? No, people shouldn't count on her attending. I rang her up a second time all the same, once everything had been agreed with the funeral parlour.

'Do you want to come?' I asked. 'Should I pick you up?'

To which she replied as if it were the most idiotic idea she'd ever heard, exclaiming, 'What?' Then there was a kind of coughing on the line. She had been overcome by a coughing fit, a hoarse cough that sounded as if she were choking to death.

She did come, though; she watched from between the firs up on the hill.

He had neglected all his friendships in recent years, so very few people came to his funeral. The neighbours, but not everyone; just one from each of the surrounding houses, one person so it looked as if they had been assigned to the funeral or the household had drawn lots—people I only vaguely knew; Frau Roth, clutching a tissue she raised to her nose every now and then; her husband, who stood staring at the tips of his shoes; and a few elderly employees from the department he had run.

We left the hall where he had been laid out on a bier and were walking behind the coffin as it rolled up the path on an electric trolley under the late-September sun when Mila nudged me.

'That's Herta, isn't it?'

A line of young fir trees ran across the hill as neatly as soldiers at roll call, and she, Herta, was standing in a gap between two trees in a shiny red dress (taffeta, Mila reckoned) and draped over the crook of her arm was a thin gabardine coat the same yellowy-red colour as the leaves of the lemon tree outside her window. I had to wait until the ceremony was over before I could go to her, so we trudged along behind the whirring cart, and she followed us. Half hidden by the row of fir trees, she walked up the hill, maintaining a constant distance (maybe 50 yards) between us, but when the funeral guests had departed and I turned to look for her, she was gone. I spotted her again after a while. Unlike the others, she wasn't heading to the main entrance but towards the home, and so I lost sight of her for a moment. I caught up with her only at the small iron gate which gave access to the cemetery from the town side.

'Mother,' I called. 'Wait.'

And now that she knew she couldn't shake me off, she stopped.

'Oh, it's you,' she said, as if she'd only just noticed me.

'So you did come after all.'

'A coincidence. Pure coincidence. I was out for a walk and just happened to be passing.'

It was important for her to stress that she attended her husband's funeral by accident.

We passed through the gate and up the path through the dry grass to the home. She stopped in the driveway and, as always, extended a stiff arm to shake my hand, then turned on her heel and walked up the gravel path to the steps without acknowledging Mila, who was standing a few paces behind us.

The only person at *her* funeral was her ward nurse—the (in her eyes) coarse woman. I spotted her first, then the director of the home as well, and the young man who had rung me. That day he was wearing not a caftan but a dark suit that was too big for him and flapped around his arms and legs. He had rubbed gel into his hair and combed it back so severely that it stuck to his scalp, with visible furrows from the teeth of his comb. He was holding in his hand (like a flag) a rose whose yellow petals shaded into red at the

A FINE COUPLE

edges. He came with the nurses but kept his distance a few paces behind them. He was clearly intent on not appearing to be part of their group.

Mila wasn't there that day; she had gone back to Berlin. That will be why these details were engraved in my memory. I wanted to describe the young man to her. Or did I think he would cause some kind of stir? An outburst? A fit of rage? At the funeral parlour, he didn't take a seat when the others sat down in the front row but stood behind the benches, scowling.

Throughout, and also during the brief graveside ceremony later, I could feel his gaze on the back of my neck, but when I looked round, he was staring at the floor. As soon as I looked away, I felt his eyes on me again. This young man, the nurse, the director of the home and me. And the vicar of course, a chubby-cheeked man who looked like my Religious Education teacher at school, and had immediately remembered me when I phoned him.

'Herr Karst,' he said. 'One so soon after the other.'

I don't think he knew my parents, though. Frau Roth had called him after Georg's death, and he in turn had rung me and enquired about the dates he should weave into his sermon. Herta, on the other hand, he would have seen many times because although she didn't attend his church, he was frequently in and out of the home. I gathered from a few comments he made that he was aware of her disappearance and her return.

As he raised his hands to deliver the blessing, two air force jets sped over the valley so low that they seemed to brush the tops of the trees of the hills on the far slope and, glancing up, I saw a rabbit in the exact spot where she had stood by the fence. And I knew that he too had come.

She had come in her dark-red taffeta dress, and he had come as a rabbit.

2

The next morning, before leaving for Tautenburg, I went up into the attic, opened the cupboard, took out the cardboard box full of pictures and looked for a photo I'd remembered when I woke up. I couldn't find it though, only a shot I had taken of it years back— a photo of a photo.

I had propped up the original against a pile of books on the balcony table and photographed it, which was why the picture now had a second coloured border outside the serrated white one. You could see the books, the edge of the table, the balcony railing, a strip of blue sky and, in the centre, the black-and-white photo of my father sitting with rolled-up shirt sleeves at his desk in the steelworks and writing something on a sheet of paper. He was looking up and laughing, as if the photographer had caught him off guard. He never liked being photographed, so this was one of the few surviving pictures of him. He had given it to me, along with a few other even older snaps, during a visit; on the few later ones he was either not alone or they had been taken from such a distance that his face was blurred.

Apart from the pictures by the Baltic Sea on their last holiday together, there are none of him with Herta. Either she had taken them with her or he had destroyed them, and even those holiday pictures can only have remained by chance.

Mila was sitting in the kitchen when I came down from the attic. She had made some coffee after getting up.

'Is that him?' she asked.

I nodded.

She took the picture from my hand and studied it. 'How old is he here?'

'Thirty-four.' I thought about this. Yes, Brandenburg, steelworks . . . he couldn't be more than thirty-four.

'That young?'

'That young.'

Mila had arrived on the evening of the first workday after Christmas. To clear out my mother's belongings . . . The director of the home had insisted I do this, and since Mila had agreed to come with me, this was the only possible week—the week between the years.

Her belongings? Well, she didn't really have any, only what was in her wardrobe: underwear, shoes, dresses and the sewing machine which, when not in use, was also stowed away in a cupboard. It had, however, been in near constant use.

Even though her contacts with the reps from whom she had purchased essentials had ended years earlier, she kept spiriting up new fabrics and would then sit hunched over the machine with a pin between her pursed lips—a pin she would take out and stick in her sleeve when I entered, always in the same place, a hand's breadth below the shoulder.

Her wardrobes overflowed with clothes made for the sort of festive gatherings she was never invited to. Or no longer, at any rate. Still she went on sewing. It was as if she was trying to prove what a wise investment the sewing machine had been. Self-imposed drudgery, I thought every time I saw her, but she didn't see it that way.

The underwear, the shoes, the clothes, the sewing machine, the ashtrays standing around all over the place and the all-glass table lamp—these were the things she had kept, along with the photos (stored in a grey envelope).

Between Christmas and New Year that was.

First her place, then his. We packed the things into a few moving boxes and when we were almost finished, the manager of the home came in and offered to keep them in the storeroom, temporarily, until we knew what to do with them.

Afterwards, we drove down the hill, through town and up the hill on the other side. It was a bright, sunny day but very cold; the streets slumbered as on a public holiday. I unlocked the front door and pulled up the venetian blinds. The light came slanting through the windows. Clear out his belongings? No, that wasn't the plan, not at his place; here, the idea was to take stock. We needed to examine the items and decide what to do with them, and because I knew I was, in a sense, gauging their usefulness, I walked around feeling as I if was engaged in some improper and reprehensible act.

While Mila tried to get the coffee machine going, I went into his study, a small room on the garden side of the house, and looked around. Pulling out a binder that was standing alongside others on a small shelf behind the desk and opening it, I found the letter that had been sent to Plothow and ought never have been sent to Plothow; and when I saw that the others—the carbons of the letters he had written, and her replies—had been filed away underneath them, I snapped the binder shut and put it in the hallway so I wouldn't forget it when the time came to head home.

That permanent sense of trespassing as I walked around, opening and closing cupboards. Then in the afternoon twilight,

16

when we'd already put our coats on, I peeked into the bedroom again. Opposite the bed was a wardrobe, a kind of fitted wardrobe running from one wall to the other, its big doors covered by smaller sliding ones. Later, I couldn't explain what made me switch on the light, climb up onto a chair and push the door to one side, and when I lifted the pile of sheets in the compartment, I saw something wrapped in a cloth and knew what it was before I even took it out.

The camera.

I say *the*, not *a*, because as I stood up there on a chair in his bedroom in Tautenburg, I knew which camera it was.

'What kind of camera is it?' Mila asked as we drove down the hill.

'An Exakta, 6 by 9 roll film, made in '57,' I replied, and I recall immediately realizing my mistake. There was no reason to mention the year; there was no telling from the camera. As if to distract her, I leant forward and, with the back of my hand, wiped the steam of our breath from the windscreen.

Sun in the morning, clouds in the afternoon, massing into sulphur-yellow mountains of cloud in the sky; now that it was dark, bands of sleet drifted towards us, each gust of wind obscuring the road as if behind a veil. Mila was driving. She sat bolt upright at the wheel, squinting and staring at the road as it wound its way down the hillside. Then, as we came to the motorway, she brought it up again.

'Why was it up there?' she asked.

'No idea.'

'Is it any good?'

'The camera?'

'Yes.'

I pretended to give this some thought. 'I think so.'

And I could have followed up by saying that I'd been toying with the idea of buying this precise camera for some time. It was cheaper than the Japanese models most people used and just as good. There was a shop in Berlin, not far from where I lived at the time, that could get hold of them. The store's owner would contact someone in East Berlin, who would buy them and smuggle them over the border. I could have done with one back then. I didn't have much money, gear was expensive, and I had to borrow a camera for my first photo reportage. But I decided not to. It was made in Dresden. What if it had got damaged?

But I didn't say that. Well, not then. Only later.

*

Superficially, nothing had changed. I would wake up early and go up to the attic after breakfast, mostly just a cup of coffee and two crispbreads, and answer letters. Sometimes I would stand by one of the pivot windows, push it open and look out over the rooftops at the planes approaching in quick succession over Offenbach and Sachsenhausen to land at Frankfurt airport. Life went on as usual. Except that when the time came to go down to the darkroom in the cellar, I would hesitate and more than once I went down, stood outside the door for a while and then turned back.

When I rang a friend, I noticed that his wife, who had come to the phone, adopted a cautious and embarrassed tone of voice, and so I told her that she could talk to me normally, after all I wasn't sick, which made her laugh; and after she had handed him the receiver, I repeated the same thing before realizing I had trouble keeping up with the conversation. My friend's words came to me as if through a sound-absorbent wall, while my own bounced strangely around my skull, as if I wasn't sitting in a room but at the bottom of a well.

This continued for several days. Whenever I spoke to someone, I found myself simultaneously listening to my words, and it always struck me as if my voice was too loud, a thundering bass filling the room, whereas it was scarcely audible to the other person. People kept saying, 'Speak up, Philipp!'

When I got good news, I reflected that I couldn't share it with him any more. In the cupboard I found a ream of loose leaves for ring binders my father had given me years earlier; in the cellar, a pair of pliers from his toolkit. Passing a mirror, I would stop and study myself, as if expecting my similarities with him to have become more pronounced. My movements were clumsy, and I often knocked things over or missed something I went to pick up. And I kept mislaying things: my lighter, my key, my wallet.

At noon, after shopping, I sat down in a cafe and ordered an espresso. Suddenly I caught myself looking at my hands and thinking, *His*. Whether it was my facial expression or my posture, my habits or tastes, the way I propped up my head on my hand while talking or crossed my legs when seated, picked up a fork or poured water—I reviewed everything and saw everything in a new and threatening light. *Like him*, I thought. *Just like him*. And when I paid and got up to go, it wasn't myself I saw walking past shop windows but him.

It had been a long time since I had suffered from any psychosomatic illness, but I now began to notice all the symptoms of his condition in myself. For weeks on end I felt a pressure in my stomach, a tugging in my left arm, and throughout this it was as if a hand were squeezing my heart.

In the evenings I would fall asleep, exhausted, and wake up again an hour later; then I would get up, sit in an armchair and try to read, but my mind would immediately start to wander, and I'd think back to how his walking around at night would sometimes wake me and in the morning the windows would be open. He opened them to get rid of the smoke. I stubbed out my cigarette, shut my book, stepped out onto the balcony, bent over and let my arms swing back and forth in front of my legs, and all at once it hit me that he used to do the same; he too had occasionally stood by the window and swung his arms back and forth to expel the smoke from his lungs.

Then, in early November, the dreams returned. There are two of them. Two dreams. I'll describe them as I noted them down at the time.

I can see them through the low-hanging branches of a willow tree. He is lying on his back, his arms outstretched as if he's asleep (or exhausted by lovemaking), their white undersides glowing. What is strange, though, is that he has a cloth over his head; his head is hidden by a cloth covering his face. She is lying alongside him, snuggled up against him, her arm across his chest as if to protect him. Her bottom is slightly raised, her left leg flung over his legs, her head on his shoulder. Thus, in this relaxed position, they sink into the ground.

That is the day dream.

I had this dream over a long period, in Plothow and then in Tautenburg, and since I knew that it was them I had seen, I woke up each time in horror. In horror because I had seen them sink into the ground, and also with shame because they were naked. I'd seen them naked and so I couldn't tell them about my dream.

I couldn't tell them either dream. When they asked me the next morning, 'What did you dream about, Philipp?' I shrugged and said, 'No idea.' But I did.

I'd had this dream as a child. Then it stopped for almost my entire adult life, only resuming after their deaths.

In the other dream it is night. It is the dream of the boy and the woman. I am looking at a room lit by a flickering light, a candle perhaps. The boy seems to be poorly and is lying on a bed or a mattress on the floor in a corner, whereas the woman is standing by the stove. She is holding a spoon in one hand, stirring a pot. She's making him something to eat, a special request because he's ill. Eventually she turns round, walks over to him and sits down on his chest. She lifts her skirt, moves forwards until she's sitting on his face and lets her skirt fall. Then she begins to bob up and down. She rides on his head, slowly at first, then faster.

When it is over, she clambers off and goes back to the stove, while the boy turns onto his side so I can see his face. One of his eyes is closed to a narrow slit, while the other is where his cheekbone should be, and with this eye he stares at me.

I had this dream too over a long period of time—not every night, but often enough to recognize it immediately on its return many years later.

First one dream, then the other.

3

Herta was a beautiful woman, and it was said when she was young that she was destined to become a model. That's what people said among themselves in Plothow. If this rumour reached her ears or someone asked her about it, she would tip her head to one side and smile in a way that left it open to interpretation whether there was any truth to it.

She was 17 or 18, tall and (people said) twig-like. She worked as a seamstress at Parvus' clothing store, although for a few years now the sign above the entrance had shown a different name— Mill, the name of the man who had seized the shop from Parvus through blackmail or by exploiting, for a ridiculously small sum of money, the misery that had befallen the man due to his Jewish roots. Parvus and his family had emigrated to the United States, to New York where he worked as a tailor for the first few years to keep their heads above water while Mill strutted around his house in Plothow and made a big show of being a businessman. But that didn't change the fact that people who shopped there still said, 'I'm off to Parvus'.' Parvus may have been driven out, but his name remained.

The owner of shares in a second clothing store in Berlin, acquired in the same way as Parvus' shop, Mill clearly had a crush on Herta, for after observing her for a while he made her a proposition. In spring and autumn, when the new collections arrived, he organized fashion shows for his female customers at the

Berlin store, not far from Wittenbergplatz. 'Would you like to take a look?' he asked.

Of course she would. She drove to Berlin with him in his car and was allowed to model clothes alongside other tall girls. She walked down the catwalk, came back behind the curtain, was put in a new dress and sent out again every Thursday afternoon for a whole spring and a whole autumn, and when the season was over Mill said to her as they waited at a level crossing, 'I've been having a think. You ought to become a model.'

She looked at him with surprise, for that was exactly what she herself had been contemplating this whole time. Ever since she had realized that this would be her last Berlin trip for a while, she had been pondering if it mightn't be possible to work there, even if it was in this strange profession. It would be different from shuffling around on her knees, pinning up hems, in the shop in Plothow.

'I'll give you a helping hand,' said Mr Mill. 'You'll start at Tauentzienstrasse, and then we'll take it from there.'

It might also have started then, I think. With that promise of a different and better life.

It was already dark. The lights of the train whooshed past. Sitting next to Mill in the car she thought, *I'm going to live in Berlin*. She told her friend Lilo, who worked in her parents' shop, and Lilo passed the news on to other friends: Herta's off to Berlin.

Suddenly, though, Mill started coming to the shop only at night. He would enter through the door in the yard and leave the same way. The curtains were drawn, but it was clear from the light that filtered around their edges that he was sitting in his office upstairs, and a few weeks later the business changed hands. The name over the entrance was replaced again. When she came to the store one morning the name above the door was Berger, and the bearer of that name was obviously an even bigger blackmailer and profiteer than Mill, who, for whatever reason, had vanished into thin air. Berger's name was emblazoned in large gold letters over the entrance.

People still said they were going to Parvus', though.

That was in December, quarter of a year before Georg first spotted her from the top of a truck.

The truck was driving along Brandenburger Strasse. He was sitting at the rear of the load bed with the tarpaulin folded back. It was around noon. He had rested his head on the tailgate and was squinting into the sun, with his hands on the railing. Having stretched out his legs, he was lying more than sitting. He loved these drives whose purpose was to move lorries from one place to another. There was a sudden lurch, and he was thrown forwards against the cab. Getting to his feet, he saw that they had crashed into a tractor reversing out of a driveway.

At that very moment she stepped out of the shop directly opposite and stopped in the doorway.

He climbed down from the load bed, ran to the front of the truck and, establishing that no one had been injured, turned to look at the girl. She was still standing in the doorway, watching. Half an hour later they were sitting opposite each other at a cafe table. Later, it was to this cafe that they would regularly come.

In the following weeks he came to Plothow more often. More often? As often as his military service allowed, and he also came when it didn't. Discussing it, he seemed surprised by such an uncharacteristic dereliction of his duties, and he would ponder for a second, as if trying to recall its cause. He would sit in a corner of the garden behind the house, out of the wind, staring at his hands.

It must have been like this: he would leave the barracks in uniform and drive to the station where he had deposited a bag of civilian clothing so that, if stopped, he wouldn't be asked for his leave pass. He took the bag from a locker and went to the toilets, locked himself in a cubicle, removed his uniform and put on the suit. He would wrap the uniform in a piece of fabric, place it in the bag and put it back in the locker. Then he would buy a ticket to Plothow and board the train.

She would be waiting for him in the cafe where they had sat after the accident.

The shop closed at six. Around half past six, after clearing up, she would come out and dawdle for a bit, looking in shop windows. It wasn't worth going home for an hour so she would wander up and down the main street or pay a visit to Lilo, whose parents ran the large radio shop at the top end of Brandenburger Strasse until, at about half past seven, she judged it was time to go to the cafe. She would sit down at a table by the window from where she could keep an eye on the street, the door through which he would enter and the clock above it.

He would come shortly after eight and sit down opposite her. They rested their hands on the table and stared at them. The tips of their middle fingers touched, then their hands moved towards each other until their other fingers met. His fingertips rested on hers. Finally, their hands advanced until they lay firmly on top of each other. She felt the coarse fabric of his trousers against her leg. As soon as it got dark, he signalled to the waitress and paid. They stepped out into the street and after crossing the bridge, went down to the canal via a flight of red brick steps so narrow that he had to go first, before taking the then unpaved towpath. To their left shimmered the black ribbon of the canal, to their right lay a park designed by a student of Lenné's—a garden with rare shrubs and trees, ponds and small humpback bridges spanning a stream. Now and then a barge puttered past. The smell of diesel hung in the air, and water lapped and gurgled against the stone embankment.

He had put his arm around her and when they thought nobody could see them from the bridge, they would stop and embrace, take a few more steps and then stop again. He ran his hand over her back and when it was completely dark and the bridge was far enough away, he drew her down the bank.

He came to Plothow every other Tuesday, but she always knew that something could crop up and she might wait in vain.

She would stare at the clock over the door and should he not be there by nine, she would know he wasn't coming and had been detained in Magdeburg. Moments earlier she had been sitting in a special cafe, but now it was special no more. She saw the tables with their grubby doilies and sticky Bakelite sugar pots, the wallpaper blackened by the stovepipe and the stupid, unevenly arranged pictures—now all the things stood out which she hadn't noticed while she was still able to count on his imminent arrival. All of a sudden, the objects had lost that special feel, revealed their true nature. And it was the same out in the street into which she stepped after settling the bill; the street had changed too. She took the same route as with him, but all of a sudden it was only Plothow she was walking through, the town she had hoped to escape with Mill's aid.

She passed the stairs leading down to the canal but, alone, she would stay on the road and only at the end of the park did she turn into the village-like part of town and the wide, cobbled street that led out to the bleaching green, a meadow almost on the edge of town, lined on one side by single-storey houses and bordered on the other by a small pine wood. As she strode towards her parents' house, she told herself that if he hadn't come today, it was because he couldn't but next time he certainly would. She felt a double yearning, one for him and one that existed even without him but which, for simplicity's sake, she referred to by his name: Georg.

Every other Tuesday, that was when she waited for him.

He generally came by train, though occasionally a friend on his way to Potsdam would give him a lift in his car. He got out at the turn-off to Havelberg and as he approached the cafe where she was sitting, he would see her through the window—her head, her neck, her narrow shoulders poking through the thin fabric—and think that she was the most beautiful thing he had ever laid eyes on. And when he came unexpectedly, at night, without having been able to warn her, he went out to the bleaching green, climbed over the fence into the front garden and knocked on the shutter, two short raps in quick succession, then a third. She slept soundly, but at this signal she would wake up. She would throw on a dress over her nightshirt, creep past her parents' bedroom, which lay on the other side of the hallway, go out through the laundry room into the yard and slide back the iron bar across the gate.

'Quietly,' she would say, 'quietly,' raising a finger to her lips.

He wore heavy boots whose heels clacked on the flagstones in the yard when he trod firmly. She would take his hand, and he followed her on tiptoes. They kept to the shadow of the cowsheds, whispered to each other and leant against the wall in the passageway leading to the garden.

'Where have you just come from?' she asked and before he could answer, she would entwine her arms around his neck and pull him down to her.

Whenever her parents knew she was meeting him, they said, 'Eleven. Be back by eleven.'

Georg was a soldier, a career soldier, on his way to becoming an officer, and they didn't like her meeting him. No more than they had liked her trips to Berlin with Mill. Which is to say: he didn't like it, her father. He wanted nothing to do with those people, whereas her mother was torn. On the one hand she admitted that her husband was right, but on the other she liked him. She had seen the boy only once, but she liked him as much as her daughter did. She liked his voice, his gangling gait, his timid manner. She didn't say so, though. She would never have said anything with which her husband didn't agree.

On Tuesday evenings they stayed up. They waited in the golden glow of the lamp hanging over the table, he reclining on the sofa behind his newspaper, she on the chair at the head of the table, busy with work she would otherwise have put off to the next day, doing needlework or shelling peas; the clock ticked, the paper rustled, the peas clattered into the brass dish—until they heard their daughter's footsteps on the sandy path skirting the meadow. When they heard her come into the hallway, he would get up, open the living room door and watch (wordlessly) as she peeled herself out of her coat and hung it on a coat peg.

Then he closed the door again.

Sixty kilometres roughly, three quarters of an hour it took Georg to get to Plothow. Three quarters of an hour there and three quarters of an hour back. He came by train, sometimes by car, and took the first train back the next morning. The carriages were full of workers on their way to the early shift in Burg or Magdeburg. He sat in a corner by the window and hoped the train would be on time. It didn't bear thinking about what would happen if he didn't make it back to barracks undetected.

He also came to Plothow when he knew he could only stay for an hour, and he came too when he could stay for longer but knew she had to be home long before his train left. He walked her out to the bleaching ground and loitered until it was time to go to the station. He had a taste for backstreets, for nooks and crannies where nobody ever came because they were so out of the way and dingy. He passed the sugar factory, the docks, walked along the small street behind the town hall where the prison was, returned to the bridge and gazed at the canal below, running straight as a die through the countryside. It didn't bother him that it was dark; anyway, it was never totally dark. The street lamps were no longer lit, but the moon shone, and the stars.

From Magdeburg it had been easy to visit her. What was a two-hour journey? But then he heard that his unit was going to be transferred to Koblenz. He came one night, unannounced, to tell her the news. They leant against the wall of the cowshed side by side and discussed what to do.

'I'll come to Koblenz,' she whispered. 'I'll visit you.'

But a month later the war her father had predicted broke out. That was why he was against these people, because war followed on their heels. This deployment—as they didn't know while they were leaning against the cowshed wall, as they could not have known— was already part of the war, and he wasn't deployed to Koblenz after all, but to the slate town where she was to set foot 18 years later.

In the two period photos (there are none of them together, though there are some of her and some of him), she has a soft face with a heavily made-up mouth and thin, plucked eyebrows arcing in semi-circles over her eyes; on one she has a middle parting and her wavy hair is combed back; on the other it is in rollers close to her head that look like spiral pastries, fastened with hairpins; on both she has her hand under her chin, but it is clear that she isn't really supporting her head but that it is a pose she may have copied from a movie poster hanging in the display case of a cinema she passed on one of her lunchtime strolls, a grey building, set back slightly from the other houses with half-columns to the left and right of the entrance, which screened films starring Lilian Harvey and Willy Fritsch, and where a Sylvester Stallone film was showing during my first visit to Plothow after the Wall opened.

The photos of her are postcard size, which automatically reminds you of portraits of actors, whereas the pictures of him from the same year are not much larger than postage stamps, which meant using a magnifying glass if you wanted to discern his features. In one, Georg is standing next to his parents, a head taller than them, in the garden of the house in Dresden; he's wearing a white jacket which makes his hair seem even darker than it was. All it took was a few rays of sunshine to turn it brown. His usually slightly wavy black hair is cropped short. His eyes are smiling, but it is a fake, melancholy smile for the photographer and the other people in the picture. Even then, he was shrouded in a sadness he never avowed to anyone.

He is standing at one end, next to his mother, leaning slightly as if to be closer to her, which immediately underscores his distance from his father. His father, a well-built man whose sternness he had joined the army to escape, is staring straight at the camera. He has struck a wide stance and has one hand on his hip, just as in another photo which shows him posing in front of his workers, like a general with his troops, after the completion of a bridge whose construction he was overseeing.

His mother, loved but helpless, has a ghost of a smile on her lips. Georg knows that Herta was already on the scene when this photo was taken, but if he told anyone, then only her.

4

I now believe that their affair began one evening when he came home later than usual. It was, I assume, a late-autumn day, at the end of November when night came early. The Hungarian uprising had occurred a few weeks earlier, but its aftershock was still rippling through people's minds. The lights were on in the kitchen. It was windy, and the branches of the horse chestnut, to which a few rust-flecked leaves still clung, were swishing outside the window.

Hearing the car that brought him home whenever he stayed at the works too late to catch the last train to Plothow, she stood up, walked along the passageway to the living room and stood by the window. She saw him get out, bend down to the car window and exchange a few words with Radinke, the driver, before turning and heading for the house. Seconds later she heard the key in the porch door, his footsteps on the stairs, and, when he entered, she told him that she was fed up.

'I'm fed up of being frightened when you come home so late. Every time, I imagine you've been arrested or are having to justify yourself to some idiots not worthy of polishing your shoes. You don't need to put up with this! Let's leave while we're still young.'

He was shocked by her forthright words. It was a sign of the fear bottled up inside her—fear, and fatigue too. It wasn't the first time she had broached the subject; she had done so before, but never so vehemently. He shut the kitchen door so that no one who happened to be using the stairs would overhear their conversation.

'Let's wait a little longer,' he said.

But she didn't want to. She was scared for him, for herself, for the boy asleep in his bedroom. And of time. Yes, she was scared of time too.

She had developed a sensitivity to time, a sense of time trickling away. She could see it in the lines she had marked on the door to chart the boy's growth, each line marking time's shrinking, and she saw it in herself. Her appearance was changing: her arms, which had once been like sticks, were growing rounder; two lines descended from her nostrils to the corners of her mouth, wrinkles were setting in under her eyes, and her soft face, still immature in the early photos, was hardening; it was perhaps only then that it became a face compared to which the previous one against which she measured it was but a larva, a pupa from which the real one was now emerging; maybe she was becoming more beautiful than before without realizing it, or if she did, then it only exacerbated her worries. In the autumn, columns of Russian tanks advanced through the town on their way to manoeuvres, ripping the cobblestones out of the streets with their treads. There was a swirl of rumours that the borders were going to close. The boy would soon be entering his second year at school. Planes flew westwards over the house, and indoors, inside the house, time passed.

'Please,' she said.

He was hesitant, but then he gave in and crossed the border. That was still possible. He wanted to see what things were like in the West, in the real West, not in West Berlin where Herta's aunt lived. Herta and the boy visited her occasionally, returning with red-hot ears, bursting with ideas. Sure, her hopes of being a model were over, but she still had an eye for fashion and could sew any dress from memory, even ones she had seen only once. Shop after shop was opening on Tauentzienstrasse. No, he wasn't going there. He had a friend who lived in Hanover and occasionally sent him news, short letters saying that he was fine. That's where he went— to Hanover, to his friend's.

Late January. An icy rain was falling.

Herta accompanied him to the station under an umbrella. She gave him a hug before he boarded the train, and as she walked back through the town, she pictured him stuck in that smoky compartment, rolling towards the unfamiliar city which she imagined to be just over the border.

She slanted the umbrella against the rain that came driving towards her in gusts, unable to see anything but the stretch of path in front of her feet, the black cobbles on the pavements, the grooved asphalt of the slope up to the bridge, the stamped, potholed sandy path through the park, and finally the lighter cobbles as she turned into her street. Huddling under the umbrella, she passed, without seeing them, all the familiar buildings— Parvus' department store (as it was still known), the picture house, the brick church, the fieldhands' low cottages and the farmers' houses with the ornamentations above their doors and windows.

Still, I thought as I walked the same route years later, even without the umbrella, she wouldn't have noticed anything. She had known the town her whole life, so she would have been blind to it, as I too became after any length of time in a town, not through heedlessness but due to familiarity.

He had planned to stay away for two days, but this stretched to three, and in those three days there was a twist she could not have foreseen.

He had signed up at 19. A professional soldier. He was 26 when the war ended, and his friends had been soldiers too. He'd met them during his stint in the army; he had no others, no one to whom he could talk about really important matters, I mean. They were dead, killed in action or missing. One of the few survivors was the man he went to see that January day.

He'd taken almost nothing with him, just the bare necessities for a day, a night and another day. He was wearing a suit and a coat, and in the briefcase he kept on his lap, for there was no room on the luggage rack, he had his shaving kit, toothbrush, soap and comb. That was all.

It rained throughout the journey and it was still raining when the train pulled into Hanover. His friend was waiting for him on the platform, to his surprise in a uniform so grey and unremarkable he took it for a security guard's. This friend only ever appeared in his accounts as the 'friend'—as a friend or a brother-in-arms—and so that's what I'll call him. After flirting with a variety of professions and failing at all of them, Major Friend had entered the newly established West German army. They drove to Friend's flat and when he told him he was considering coming to the West, Friend said, 'Join us then.'

'You?' he asked.

'Yes, us.'

He'd heard those words once before, at the steelworks where he worked. Not half a year back, two men had walked into his office and said, 'Join us. We need people like you.'

They were wearing the uniform of the Barracked People's Police which wasn't yet an army or, if it already was, wasn't yet known as such, and when they had left again, Kabusch, the party secretary at the works, came in and said the same: 'You have to, Georg. It's your duty.'

Kabusch was a man who put his big meaty hands on his knees when seated. I'd met him. He had visited us once in Plothow, which is when I'd seen his hands, resting there like hunks of meat on his knees, I recalled. With his big hands Kabusch sat opposite him and said, 'It's your duty, Georg.' He said it that day, and every time they met in the days that followed he said, 'Georg!'

But he didn't want to. Or not any more. And finally, when Kabusch wouldn't stop pestering him, he went to see a doctor he knew well and who, more importantly, was friends with the works doctor, who would of course need to be consulted, and the two of them wrote a certificate stating that he was sick (heart, lungs) and unfit for military service, not any more, and he presented this certificate to Kabusch.

That's how he had wriggled his way out of the situation in Plothow, but now, in Hanover, he was caught in two minds.

If, he thought, *if we do* . . . then wouldn't it be sensible to weigh up Friend's proposition? And while he was still thinking, the other man said, 'I know what we'll do.'

'Now?'

'We'll drive to Bonn.'

'To Bonn?'

'Yeah. To the ministry.'

And so that's what they did. The next morning, they drove to Bonn in Friend's car. The whole journey he thought it was a mistake, but then he calmed down, telling himself, *Wait and see, none of this is binding.* They passed through the Weserbergland. Was that the Porta Westfalica? Is that snow up there? And is that Bielefeld? The outskirts of the Ruhr region. Grim nods.

They crossed the Rhine near Cologne; the windscreen wipers hummed. Most of the time Georg held a soft leather cloth to wipe the glass which kept steaming up with their breath.

They climbed the stairs to the personnel department, Friend in uniform, he in civilian clothes; and after he'd talked to a few people in the same uniform as Friend's he thought the same as he had in Plothow: *No, this is not for me*. He didn't say it out loud, though; he kept it to himself. As if to leave himself an escape route (or to avoid making Friend look like a braggart in front of these people for having dragged in someone who wasn't interested in their proposals), he listened to everything and nodded. Only when they were going back down the stairs did he shake his head.

'What do you mean?' Friend said, looking at him. But he stuck to his decision.

'No,' he said. 'Sorry.'

They drove back to Hanover, and Friend dropped him off at the station. Friend was so disappointed in him that they exchanged no more than two or three words during the journey. Friend let him out but didn't bother getting out himself. By the time Georg turned to wave, Friend had disappeared around a corner. It was about 11 at night, the last train to Magdeburg had long since departed, and so he went into the waiting room and sat down on a bench. He slept like that, his briefcase on his lap, and travelled home to Plothow the next morning.

The story might well have ended there, but it was in fact only the beginning. That was how he saw it, anyway. For him the story started with the letter that arrived in Plothow a few weeks later, whereas I think it began far earlier, with his indecision, with his attempt to keep all options open, even though he knew that the one Friend was offering him was off limits.

Or did it begin with her fear for him? Not about the letter but about the nights he didn't come home because he was stuck at work? There was a constant stream of meetings lasting into the early hours which were only superficially about achieving or missing targets, procuring spare parts, delivery problems, etc. The constant aim of these meetings was to search for a scapegoat who could, in the (likely) event of failure, be flagged up to the party leadership in Berlin without identifying the true culprit, whom Kabusch was also aware of (he wasn't stupid).

The fear that drove her to say: We have to get out of here. The fear may also have been the beginning, a fear inspired by her love for him, so that it could perhaps be said that it was her love that destroyed her love.

And what about you? I asked her once when she seemed approachable. Your glances in the mirror? Your nostalgia for Tauentzienstrasse? But she was already looking elsewhere, gave no answer.

Anyway, they cancelled their escape. It was over before it had even begun.

And that was fine by him, I think.

He didn't want to leave. He believed (despite the fears he too harboured) that he had found a home. He had only ever lived in places for short spells, in the village near Metz where he was born, then in Pirna, Dresden and, after leaving home, in various garrison towns and, lastly, in different theatres of war (he couldn't be said to have 'lived' there), and he believed that was all behind him now.

Georg had been a soldier for eight years, six of them during the war, and perhaps it's true, what he said—that he'd only signed up because his father and grandfather had been career soldiers too, and he could indeed imagine doing a different job, a proper job. Admittedly, he had to think when I asked him what kind of job, before mentioning jobs that people of his class who didn't join the army always mentioned. He hesitated for a second and then said, 'Vet, forester, maybe'—looking out into the garden where we were sitting—'a farmer.' But that hadn't been an option.

In any case: he had always lived in different places, on the move. Now, in Plothow, he had a flat of his own for the first time. They had chosen and bought the furnishings together; he wasn't surrounded by someone else's furniture but by his own belongings. He slept in his own bed, hung his clothes in his own wardrobe; the window had a view of the garden and the adjacent field; people recognized him in the street, said hello to him. That too was a new experience.

Maybe he was more attached to Plothow then than his wife was, having always lived in the town and always longed to go somewhere else. She was the one who wanted to leave and who badgered him, and he was the one who gave in, and maybe this was what he remembered when he came out of prison and learnt to whom—or rather, to what—he owed his release.

5

So they stayed.

But then the letter arrived. It was lying on the table one morning. He saw it the moment he stepped into the porch. Someone had picked it up and put it on the table.

This was not unusual. There were three tenants in the building. They knew one another, albeit not well. They saw one another in the courtyard and on the stairs. They came into the house through the porch and went out into the street through the porch. If they happened to meet there, they would sit down at the table for a moment and talk about house-related matters.

The postman came around ten and tossed the mail through the slit in the door. It fell on the floor, and the first person who saw it lying there would pick it up and place the letters not addressed to them on the table, which is what someone had done with this letter.

There was only one there—a blue envelope with a red stamp on it that immediately caught his eye. The top left-hand corner was marked *For delivery only in the Federal Republic of Germany and West Berlin*, and turning the letter over, he saw the sender's name: Federal Ministry of Defence.

This letter had been sent to Plothow, to his home address. The Stasi people at the border had looked at it. Mail sorters had held it in their hands; the postman had taken it and tossed it through the door slit; someone had seen it lying on the floor, picked it up and put it on the table.

The door leading to the staircase was open, so was the door to their flat, and he could hear his wife walking around inside. He pulled the door shut, sat down on a chair and tore open the envelope.

He had stayed at home that day. Maybe that was why they hadn't arrested him yet. He hadn't gone to the works because he had a funeral to attend. If he had gone to the works, Kabusch would have called him to his office under some pretext and asked him to take a seat, and then two men in plain clothes would have entered with barely a sound and stood by the door.

Kabusch would have put his hands on his knees, leant forward and looked at him, and while his boss discussed the certificate, the heart defect, the shadow on his lung, the other two men would have stood by the door behind him without intervening. He would have known they were there, but they would have acted as if they weren't, and that would have made him even more acutely aware of their presence. Later, when the conversation turned to the West, they too would start asking questions. They would pull up two chairs and sit down beside him, one to his left, the other to his right. At some stage Kabusch would leave, and he would be alone with them.

It was mid-April, but it was already warm. The sun was shining. The porch was glazed on all sides, and the sun heated the small space like a greenhouse. The wreath he was going to take to the funeral was leaning against the wall, and in the heat the flowers interwoven with the fir twigs gave off a sweet fragrance that took his breath away. The whole porch was filled with the sickly smell.

It was morning. The funeral was that afternoon at two o'clock. By now they must have noticed that he hadn't shown up at the works. They would ask Frau Busch, his secretary, if she knew where he was. And she would answer: At home.

'He's taken the day off because he has to go to a funeral.'

So, he thought, *they're on their way.* The works were 23 kilometres from Plothow. Should he actually go to the funeral, or would it be more sensible to wait here? Yes, that might be better. Otherwise, they might come to the cemetery, and he didn't want that. It was a good acquaintance of theirs who was being buried— no, a friend—and Lilo, the widow, was his wife's best friend, and it would surely be best to wait for them here if he didn't want a disturbance at the funeral.

But when they still hadn't showed up to fetch him by midday and when half past one came and, with it, time to set off, he went after all and for the very reason that had made him consider staying at home. It wasn't just anybody who was being buried; it was Günter, Lilo's husband. He couldn't just stay at home. And if they hadn't turned up yet, they might well have postponed it by a day so as not to arrest him here in Plothow, where it would cause a stir, but at the works. He was an important figure in the administration, a Party member, deputy director, and that might have influenced their deliberations. That was how it looked.

He put on his dark suit, his wife her black dress, and as they were about to leave the flat (she was already standing in the doorway), he went back inside, entered the living room and looked around.

The letter was lying on the table. It couldn't stay there. But where should he put it? Burn it? No, that would be stupid. He opened the cupboard and pulled out the drawers. Should he put it in the compartment with his personal documents or hide it among the photos or, perhaps better, beneath the underwear in the bedroom wardrobe. In the end he lifted up the carpet, slipped it underneath and placed a chair exactly on top of the letter.

'What are you doing in there?' he heard her call from the porch.

'I'm coming,' he said, more to himself than anything, and glanced around again. He suddenly thought hiding the letter might be the stupidest thing he could do. No one knew when they would come and even *if* they would come. If they did come and find it there, though, it would be equivalent to an admission of guilt. He pulled the letter out again, put it on the table and pushed the newspaper over it. That way it wasn't immediately visible. It was covered by the paper they subscribed to, the *Volksstimme*, as if accidentally. He went into the hallway and out into the stairwell and locked their front door.

She was waiting for him in the porch. She had sat down. She was sitting at the table where the letter had lain that morning, her hands folded in her lap, calm, almost trancelike, gazing out into the garden and the adjoining field.

'Come on,' he said, picking up the wreath leaning against the wall, and they went out through the front garden into the street where they encountered other people, more friends of their friend, also dressed in black. They nodded to one another. In one hand he held the wreath, with the other he clutched her arm. She felt his hand close around it and then, perhaps to avoid the impression that he was supporting her, she shook off his hand and linked arms with him.

And so, maintaining their distance from the others so it was easier to confer, they walked through the town, the more village-like part of the town, to the cemetery. He glanced around as they spoke quietly. Maybe they were waiting until the next day, but nothing was certain.

As they passed the school their boy attended, Herta slipped her hand under his arm and rested her head on his shoulder.

'What if,' she said, without looking up, 'you stayed at home tomorrow as well?' What if she rang the works from the post office the next morning and said he was ill.

'Then they'll come for me at the flat.'

She was silent for a while. 'And what if,' she then said, 'no one noticed the letter? If neither the sender nor the red stamp caught anyone's eye?'

He shook his head. They both knew that that was out of the question. A blue letter with a red stamp. It must have caught some-one's eye at the central sorting office. Or even earlier, at the border. No doubt about it.

But then why had it been delivered? Why hadn't they just arrested him? Were they giving him a chance? Were they waiting to see if he'd take it to the party leadership and say, 'Look what arrived at my house today, comrades? Isn't it monstrous? A provocation? An attempt to split me from you?' Would that dis-tract them from the truth?

'Yes,' she said, 'that's probably right. But then you shouldn't have opened it,' she immediately added.

'Yes, then I shouldn't have opened it.'

Now that he had opened it, it looked as if he hadn't been remotely surprised to receive a letter from Bonn, and as if it had only been in hindsight, after reading it, that he'd become aware of the dangers it represented. So, what did it say?

Under the letterhead was his address and then: *Dear Herr Karst, I have happy memories of our conversation and, after consulting our senior department head, would be delighted if you would submit your CV and references as soon as possible.*

Followed by a few vacuous phrases, signature (illegible), rank.

Was it possible to talk his way out of this? Your CV and references; our conversation. There it was in black and white. It wasn't just the fact—suspicious enough—that he'd travelled to the West but he had also been in Bonn, at the defence ministry; he had talked to the enemy. Or was it better to claim that he'd met the man who had written this letter, this lieutenant-colonel, here in East Germany? That wouldn't make things any better. Quite the opposite.

No, he couldn't wheedle his way out of this fix.

They walked to the cemetery, and on the way there the decision they had been putting off for so long was made. They hadn't talked about it since his return from Hanover, and the topic had lain dormant, but now it was clear. He had to get out. To West Berlin. Not at some unspecified point in the future as they'd discussed before his trip to Hanover, but now. There was no more time to mull it over; that time had gone and the postponed decision had been taken out of their hands. They had to act right away—or, if not right away, when they got back from the cemetery. But how? If the letter had been let through to test him (as it must have been), then he was under surveillance; his every step was being watched.

He drew her closer. Pressing against his side the arm she had tucked hers under, he hugged Herta as tightly as possible as they walked. Her closeness comforted him. She made him invisible, for a moment at least and in a different way than later, when he really did become invisible, in the slate town, in the weeks following their separation. He looked down at their feet, then up again. Behind them walked the shopkeeper with the store next to the post office, and the vet, both of them with their wives. He knew this without looking round. And ahead of them were the teacher, the painter-decorator, the publican of the Lime Tree, all good acquaintances of theirs; they stared at these men's black backs. It was going to be a large funeral. Günter, the owner of an electrical store he'd taken over from his wife's parents, had been popular. Knowing him could reduce the waiting time for a television; and now Lilo, his widow, would continue to run the shop with the support of her nearly adult stepsons. No, none of these people walking to the cemetery with them was observing him. He knew them all. Everyone here observed everyone, but not in the way he now understood observation.

They walked through the April sunshine past the low houses. A black procession. He was carrying the wreath. Herta kept her arm linked with his and her head on his shoulder. They spoke quietly.

'Is it sensible for you to come along?' she asked without looking up.

'What do you mean?'

'What if they don't wait until tomorrow and send someone today instead?'

'Whom would they send?'

'Radinke, for example. What if he comes to fetch you now?'

Radinke? Yes, he did occasionally turn up without warning to take him, the comrade deputy director, to a hastily arranged meeting, sometimes in the evening, late at night, or at the weekend. He would be standing there with his worried, hangdog look when Herta opened the door and say, 'I'm sorry, Frau Karst, but . . . '

'No, not Radinke,' he parried.

'You think they'll tell him the meeting's just an excuse to lure you to the works?'

Of course not. He knew that too.

So, what then? What did she suggest? Should he turn back, pack his stuff and run away to West Berlin? Yes, he should. He should go back right now.

'But I can't,' he said.

'Why not?'

Now he looked round. Correct: the shopkeeper and the vet. She read his mind. She knew what he was thinking: these people.

'You might be feeling ill,' she said. 'That's it—you're sick.'

'What about Lilo?'

'I'll explain.'

He hesitated. 'How about you?' he asked. 'And the boy?'

'We'll follow.'

'When?'

'In a few days.'

He felt her arm move; she was trying to pull it away. Something else occurred to him. He tensed his arm and held her tight. Hadn't they said that if they had let the letter through to test him, then they must have been observing him for some time now? Or else, if it was too difficult to observe him here where everyone knew each other, they'd be watching the eye of the needle through which he might slip—the railway station? Yes, that was most likely.

They were waiting for him there. That's where they would intercept him.

'And if not?' she said. 'What if they're not?'

But then she agreed he was right. They'd catch him at the ticket office. Or wait until he boarded the train and then get on too, into the same compartment or a different one. They might travel with him incognito and reveal their identity at the final moment, perhaps in Potsdam where he had to change onto a suburban train, or later, at the last station before the West. It would be even worse then, and it was already bad enough. The letter showing he had offered his services to the enemy's armed forces. What was that called? Preparing to commit high treason? He had planned to defect with all the knowledge he had acquired in the inner circles of power, in the upper echelons of heavy industry, at conferences and among the chiefs of staff. 'Preparing'? Why play down the importance of this affair? High treason would be the charge. What had they discussed at the ministry of defence in Bonn? Joining the West German army. What else? How much secret intelligence had he revealed? And how many conversations had there been before this one—in Hanover, Bonn or here in East Germany—prior to the letter unmasking him as what they now regarded him as?

No, it would be better not to turn back. It wasn't so easy. She kept her arm threaded through his, her free hand stroking his arm and his hand, which resting on his chest as his elbow was bent. And they carried on walking.

It was a *danse macabre*, I thought the afternoon he told me this story, and now, many years later, I still think that. This clutching, releasing, drawing closer and pushing away was like a dance of the dead, and the path from the flat to the cemetery was its stage. They were still alive, they were together, they held each other's arms, but a third character was walking between them—Farewell. It was Farewell that had linked arms with them. Or was it, as I sometimes think, Death. What did you get for high treason? What was the punishment? How many years? 10? 20? Or the ultimate and greatest punishment of all? You have to bear that in mind to understand what happened next. In the slate town.

But they haven't got that far yet.

6

A radiant April day, early afternoon, very bright, then twilight, cool, the pungent smell of the decorative flowers inside the chapel. The coffin at the far end, opposite the entrance. They walk down the aisle and stop, her arm through his, then he steps away from her, lays the wreath and smooths the ribbon so the inscription is legible: A last salute. Always in our hearts. And after he takes a pace back, they are side by side once more.

She's no longer as slim as she was when they said she would be a model, but—as is plain to see in the strip of light slanting through the doors—she still has nice legs and slender ankles. She's wearing a dress she made herself, and he is in a black suit that's a little too big for him. He has lost weight; he works too hard. His black hair is slicked back. He's a head taller than her, and his back is so straight you'd think he's swallowed a stick.

They stand completely still for a moment with the eyes of the people in the chapel trained on them. Before them is the coffin. Behind them the rows of chairs are gradually filling up, a scraping of feet, whispers. And inside them fear beats its tattoo.

This is the moment when I can see them most clearly; this is the image in which their vulnerability is most acute. I watch them, side by side, through the eyes of others, the eyes of the people in the chapel. I wasn't there, but I see them as those people saw them: a fine couple. Standing in the half-darkness. Then the picture dissolves, they turn around and thread their way into the second row of chairs; Lilo, Günter's wife, and Günter's almost adult sons from his first marriage are sitting in the front row; they sit down in the row behind them, on the chairs marked with their names. They sit next to each other, her left leg pressing against his right, her left shoulder against his right, the fingers of her left hand interlinked with those of his right. It is a bit like the evening they first met. They don't wish to part just yet, but they know they must. They met in 1939 and married in 1942. He has lived in Plothow since 1945, longer than in any previous place, with the exception of Dresden, the city where he picked up his (now almost imperceptible) accent. So this is the last day. The summers rush past him, and the winters.

He hears a noise from the doorway and looks round, but it is only young Berkamp, who has arrived late and stays standing by the door, his back against the wall. No, here in the chapel he is safe.

And now, as he feels his wife's nails boring into the heel of his hand, he ponders how to organize the escape, this time in practice, not only as an idea. In front of him sits Lilo, flanked by Günter's sons who, just turned 16 and 18, already have their father's stocky frame, the same broad skulls resting, in the absence of any neck, directly on their torsos, and the same strawberry-blond hair. Peering between the elder son and Lilo, he spots the vicar, who has entered through a side door.

What should he do?

Provided, indeed, that anything can still be done. That they aren't already waiting outside. (Outside no longer means simply outside the chapel, outside the cemetery or in the street, but everything outside this room with the coffin at the back.) What then? But then he sees Lilo again, her head, the back of her neck, the hat over her pinned-up hair, a bit of the veil that flutters upwards when she breathes out and is drawn to her face when she breathes in again—Lilo, flanked by these hulking stepsons with their blockish heads and red, wiry hair, and his thoughts get no further.

He knows he is safe for the duration of the service. But when the time comes to file out behind the coffin with Günter inside, he looks around. When they step out of the chapel he cranes his neck to peer over the mourners' heads. Is there a stranger loitering among the graves, or over there in the shadow of the brick wall? No, no one there. Through the slatted gate in the wall he can see that the street beyond is empty—as far as he can tell from here, anyway. The bell tolls continuously as the procession moves away from the chapel towards the grave. It sounds like someone beating a tin bucket with a wooden stick. It sounds dull, pathetic. It's warm. The sun is still shining, and it's almost summery already. It is high time to dig the garden, but that's not going to happen now.

They walk behind Lilo and the two boys, who have obviously squeezed themselves into their confirmation suits. This is the first time he has ever seen them in suits. With every step it looks as if they're about to burst out of their clothing. Their hair is lighter out here in the afternoon light. No longer simply red, it is light blond with a tinge of red. Walking behind them, their similarity to Günter has never struck him so starkly. Until a few years ago they lived with their mother. When Günter took them in, they were no longer children but teenagers, apprentices who were clad in grey overalls whenever he saw them. Lilo, who is just as tall—taller actually in her pumps and hat—looks small and frail between them.

Then they're there. The bearers set down the coffin on the planks over the hole. They are standing with their backs to the entrance now, and he feels Herta, her arm again hooked through his, turn

51

round. She is too short, though; they're standing at the front and behind them are all the others, who have positioned themselves like a wall between them and the entrance. There is no chance of her seeing over their heads. He waits a little longer, then, as the vicar begins to speak, he turns his head and looks Gönnerwein in the face. His neighbour gives him a nod, as if to say: Yes, life is like this—it ends in death. He returns the nod, if only to shake off Gönnerwein's doleful gaze, which is glued to him. You're right, Gönnerwein. However, his view of the entrance through which they would come is obscured. Now, he thinks, now is when they're going to step out from behind the wall. And, as he hears the vicar say, 'Let us pray,' he bows his head. Raising it again he sees, far away, at the other end of the cemetery, a boy sitting on the wall and he thinks it might be Philipp; of course it's him. He nudges Herta, but the boy has vanished and he's no longer sure.

They still haven't turned up when they get home from the cemetery. There is no car waiting in front of the door, no one lurking near the house. Over the town hangs the lunchtime silence when a car is audible from several kilometres away. Herta stops by the garden gate, squints along the street and listens out. They cross the small front garden and go up the steps. The neighbour's cat is curled up on the mat outside the porch door. He bends down and lifts the animal onto the wall running along one side of the steps. It raises its head for a second, then curls up again and goes back to sleep. He unlocks the front door, and they cross the porch and go up the stairs to their flat.

Here too it is quiet. Extremely quiet. The boy went to his grand-parents' after school; Herta asked her mother to look after him for the afternoon. The first thing Georg does is open the living room door, walk over to the table and lift up the newspaper. Yes, it's there, the letter. The stamps on the letter stare up at him every bit as menacingly as they did when he was searching for a hiding place before the wedding.

That morning he had intended to wait for them because he thought they must be on their way. He wanted to be arrested here, in the flat, but when they still hadn't showed up at 1.30, he went to the cemetery and the decision was made on the way there: he would neither wait for them here nor would he hand himself in the next day.

In the chapel his mind was blank, but now—what should he take along? The suitcase? The bag? Isn't it too risky to cross town in broad daylight with a suitcase? If he did everyone would know he was going away. Where's Karst going in April? And what about the station? Hadn't they agreed it would be under surveillance? It'd be good to have a car right now. But he doesn't have one; he doesn't have a car. Of the people he trusts only Günter had a car, but Günter was dead, Lilo couldn't drive and, despite being able to drive (Günter had taught them), Günter's sons hadn't passed their driving test and were too young to justify getting them involved. As little luggage as possible, then. Just the bag. People are used to the bag. He takes it to the station every day. It's the bag in which he carries documents home to work on and, in a separate compartment, his breakfast. This is the way people know him, this is how they see him going to the station every morning and coming home every evening—when the works' car doesn't drop him off, that is.

She stands at the living room window while he gathers his things. First Wille walks past, then Berkenzien. She reports every passerby out in the street. The window is shut and she's standing behind the net curtain, slightly to one side (just in case people can see through it), but the boy's bedroom window is open. It looks out over the courtyard. If someone she doesn't know approaches the house, someone looking the way these people look, or if an unfamiliar car stops in front of the house, Georg is to jump down into the courtyard, climb over the fence and run across the field to the woods; if it's only Radinke who pulls up, however, he is to shut the door and keep quiet. She's confident she can deal with Radinke.

'I'm sorry,' she will say, 'but my husband has left for the works. How are you, Radinke?'

She won't invite him into the flat but she will sit down with him in the porch for a moment and try to find out how much he knows.

'Who sent you? Kabusch? If my husband had guessed you were coming, he wouldn't have needed to take the train. Is it something important?'

That is more or less the conversation she imagined as she kept an eye on the street and when she turns round, she notices her husband is still wearing the black suit. He's dashing between rooms in his funeral outfit.

The bag is leaning against the footboard of the bed. It doesn't hold much. Each time he puts in something essential he immediately removes it again because something else, something more important, has occurred to him. The wardrobe doors are wide open. He sees the summer suit he had made a year ago, beside it the shelves of shirts and sweaters and, on the coat stand out in the hallway, the winter coat tailored from such hard-wearing fabric that he thought it would last for 10 more years at least. It's hanging there still from the winter, which only ended a month ago; it snowed into March. These things will have to stay here, but that's unimportant. But what is important? His birth certificate, his work references and insurance documents—in short, anything with stamps and sealing wax that testifies to his 38 years of life. He must take those along, and not only those but also all proof of his parents' births, lives and deaths, as well as the letters, pictures and small objects that have been his for as long as he can remember and have become part of him. Penknife, lighter, travel alarm clock, tiepin—all the little things that have become talismans and whose loss would spell lost happiness.

He collects everything together, stuffs it into the bag, takes it out again when he realizes the bag is too heavy and puts it back on the chest of drawers where he had piled it. The only thing he pockets is the lighter—a wedding gift from his brother who was killed in action in Africa. He slips it into his trouser pocket and then forgets about it; when he changes, it stays in his funeral trousers. Then he's ready—his bag is packed. But what should he do with the letter? He'd love to rip it up and flush it down the toilet, but that wouldn't be smart. Incriminating here, it will be useful over there. It will be evidence in his favour over there, in the same way that it is evidence against him here.

The idiot whose stupidity, carelessness or calculation has disrupted his life is going to get an earful. He'll be relieved of his duties and put out to pasture; of that he can be sure.

He's startled when Herta calls his name, and rushes into the other room.

She's still standing by the window. She has opened it a fraction. That way, she thinks, she can hear what's going on outside better. She isn't satisfied with seeing; she has to hear too. She has parted the net curtain slightly, holding it in place with her right hand. She looks as if she's forgotten to let go again.

'Rita just got home,' she says and waves him over.

When he's next to her, she whispers, 'Shouldn't I send her to Mum's?'

'Why?'

'It's nearly five,' she says and, since he doesn't answer, she adds, 'I told her we'd get back from Lilo's at five.'

The boy's absence has been bugging him the whole time. It's confusing him, disorientating him. He can't leave without saying goodbye.

'Why?' he says.

'It's better,' she whispers, tilting her head towards the window as if she's heard something, maybe a car turning into their street.

'What's better?'

'It's better he isn't here.'

He thinks about this and agrees with her. Yes, she's right. How would they explain the situation to the boy? She can tell him that his father has gone away when he gets back from school tomorrow. But now? If they do turn up, should Philipp really witness his father jumping out of the window, clambering over the fence and running away across the field?

'Yes,' he says, 'you do that. Send them to your mother's.'

'OK, stay here,' she replies, all of a sudden at the same volume as he has spoken. As if it was a relay, she hands him the corner of the net curtain she was clutching and sits down at the table to write to her mother. *Dear Mum, please keep Philipp at yours for the night.*

She folds the piece of paper and hurries out.

He watches her cross the street. She is still wearing the black dress and black tights, their seams a little crooked. In her black dress, black shoes and black tights with slightly twisted seams she crosses the street, knocks on the front door opposite and goes inside straight away, only to reappear in the doorway immediately with Rita. She pats the girl on the back, and Rita heads off along the street with her rolling gait, clutching the piece of paper in her swinging hand. When Rita stops and looks back, Herta gives her an encouraging wave. They must be careful. She isn't quite right in the head. She's fine to run errands but she mustn't be cajoled too much or she turns petulant. *Go on now*, he thinks, *go*. She's standing in the middle of the street, legs akimbo, waving the piece of paper above her head. At last she turns and walks away, more slowly than before. Herta watches her go and comes back across the road, glancing up at the window and narrowing her eyes, as if she were checking whether it's possible to see through the net curtains.

Shortly afterwards he hears the porch door, then the front door and once Herta has taken up her position by the window again, he goes outside.

The bikes are leaning against one another in the shed—the boy's slightly smaller bike, Herta's, then his; his at the back. He moves the other two over to the far wall, pushes his bike out into the courtyard and wipes the saddle with his hand. He now knows what he has to do. He hasn't planned it, but now he knows. As soon as it gets dark, he must ride to Brandenburg. There's no alternative. If what they believe—that they'll be waiting for him at the station here—is true, then he has to board the train there, in the next town. He pushes the dynamo against the rim, lifts the back wheel and spins it with his palm. The lamp flickers. Good, it's working.

He leans the bike against the shed and goes into the garden beyond the yard. The walnut tree, the chestnut, the cherry tree, the three low apple trees with their whitewashed trunks, the beds surrounded by carnations and snapdragons in summer; lettuces, carrots, radishes, strawberries. He flips up his collar. It's no longer as warm as it was at midday; the sun is hanging over the field in a blue band of haze. There's the smell of freshly tilled soil. *They won't come now*, he thinks. Next, he thinks that it will be dark soon and that they tend to come when it's dark. Now, though, he is outside, the smell of soil, the smell of the canal, the resinous smell of pine, and outside, in this mellow air, it is hard to imagine being pulled back into that other world, the world of cramped rooms and bolted offices where misfortune is made.

He takes a deep breath as he passes the beds. He fills his lungs as if to stock up on air. Reaching the fence, he turns back. The first-floor lights are already on, whereas it is completely dark behind their windows.

When Herta hears the door click shut, she looks up and sees him walk along the passageway. The bathroom door, the sound of water pouring into the bath—he isn't running a bath but washing himself over the tub—, his footsteps in the bedroom. She follows his progress around the flat with one ear while listening out for noises from the street with the other; the curtains are drawn, but the window is slightly ajar. Soon afterwards he joins her, no longer in his black suit but in the grey one she laid out for him on the bed, sits down at the desk, opens the drawer and takes out the red membership booklet, puts it in an envelope and addresses it: *To Comrade Kabusch.*

He then takes a sheet of paper and writes: *Dear Walter, whatever suspicions you might have about me, I am not a traitor.*

That mattered to him. The idea of being remembered as a traitor has been tormenting him all this time. And when this too is done, he slides the blue letter with the red stamp on it into his back trouser pocket so that he doesn't forget it and turns towards her. This marks the beginning of the time they both agree was worse than anything else that day, before or after—the hour between not-yet-really-dark and totally-dark; the waiting time. He is still there, but in his mind he is already out in the street.

This image too, of them sitting there opposite each other, each in an armchair, beyond the pool of light cast by the table lamp, in the barely illuminated half of the room (which emerges before my eyes as if from a dense fog); them moving closer until their knees are touching, stretching out their arms and holding hands. I can see them in this picture too, and you could maybe say that all this storytelling has one purpose: to preserve pictures not captured on film.

They sit like this for a long time, in silence, then at his nod they get up and go down the staircase and out into the courtyard where his bike is propped up.

7

Later I rode the same route.

For a while the road runs alongside the canal and by day you can see it shimmering between the trees, pines, birches and locust trees until the individual trees thicken into woods that obscure the water and suddenly, when the woods thin out again, it's gone.

A strong wind was blowing. I bent low over the handlebars and pedalled harder.

A small cluster of houses Georg passed shortly after leaving Plothow is called Dunkelforth, then there is more woodland on either side of the road, and at some stage Plaue, a little town connected to Brandenburg by tram. The tracks wend their way between the houses and, from the edge of the town, run alongside the once-more-straight road into Brandenburg; to the left is the river Havel, to the right the lake he rowed on with Herta when she was pregnant with Philipp. Soon afterwards, like a giant pile of scrap metal with a tangle of pipes creeping up the outside of it, comes the plant where he worked or rather, on the night he rode past it, used to work—a pulsating, fire-spewing monster for smelting steel. The sky above the blast furnaces is fiery red, and columns of black smoke belch from the chimneys.

As he glanced over at the administrative wing, he noticed that the lights were on in his office and in Kabusch's on the same floor. It was half past nine; yes, Kabusch did sometimes stay very late at the works. But the fact that the lights were on in his office too could mean only one thing: the people in charge of security at the plant were searching his cupboards and desk, or else they had moved the meeting to decide his fate from Kabusch's room to his, where they were now sitting and considering what should become of him.

He was wearing the grey suit—flared trouser legs he'd fastened above the ankles with clips so they wouldn't get caught in the spokes, a sweater and the jacket over it. Rolled up on the bike rack, his grey raincoat. The briefcase dangled from the handlebars. On his feet he wore the same sturdy shoes he had worn to the funeral. I was in jeans, a polo shirt, a thin windbreaker and trainers.

He rode a heavy men's bike with a backpedal brake and a hand-operated brake that a tug would bring stamping down on the front wheel. The dynamo wheel hummed on the wheel rim. I had a light 10-gear bike and yet I still had to strain along the straight stretch leading into town past the stadium.

The road was wider here, and the wind struck me head on. *It's nearly ten*, I told myself. *You'd better get a move on if you want to make the train to Potsdam. Don't forget it's the last one.*

It was nearly six by the time I reached the station. I locked my bike to a lamppost and went into the building.

As on the evening he came in here, only one of the four counters was open, and there was long queue. I stood in line but when it was almost my turn, I peeled off, just as he had done. He'd suddenly spotted a second person behind the man at the counter studying everyone who bought a ticket. He turned and went out again, along the station building and the fence. Heavy clouds came scudding in on the wind and a few raindrops fell, harbingers of the full-on shower that set in shortly afterwards.

The streetlamps cast circles of light on the path and once past them, he climbed over the fence and ran past the bike sheds and across the tracks—the stones slewed away, clattering, under his shoes—to the platform for the train to Potsdam, clutching the briefcase and the rolled-up coat, the blue letter snug in his back pocket.

I took an easier route. I went down the steps and through the underpass. The walls were sprayed with graffiti and the odour of soot still lingered there, even though the age of the steam locomotive was long gone. I walked to the end of the platform and wondered where he might have stood before, at the last moment, jumping on the train that would carry him to Potsdam where he could take the subway to West Berlin.

I also retraced the route Herta had taken that evening.

I caught the train back. It had taken me one-and-a-half hours by bike, whereas the train covered the stretch in 20 minutes, with stops in Wusterwitz and Kirchmöser. I rode the bike to the hotel, locked it to one of the bike racks and then walked out to her flat, following the main road to Jerichow and Havelberg for part of the way. It was almost nine by the time I got there. The house in Waldstrasse was dark, and the blinds (which hadn't yet been installed back then) were down. The garden gate was shut.

After they had crossed the front garden to the street, Georg didn't mount his bike immediately but wheeled it along the pavement for a while, only swinging his right leg over the saddle and pushing off with the other one at the junction of Brettinerstrasse and Waldstrasse.

Herta stood in the gateway and watched him go. She heard the creaking of the chain and waited for the light to come on, but nothing brightened the darkness. He was riding without lights; only occasionally did she pick up the dull gleam of the reflector. She listened out for a moment and then went inside to fetch her coat.

Unlike me, she walked down Waldstrasse to the manor whose barn had burnt down to its foundations the previous year, through its grounds, over the canal bridge into Mühlenstrasse and along it to Brandenburgerstrasse where her friend lived. There was a sign on the shop door: *Closed for mourning.* The gate into the yard was bolted, and the doorbell disconnected, so she did what she used to do as a little girl: she pounded on the gate with her fists, and soon afterwards she heard Lilo's voice saying, 'What's going on?'

'It's me.'

'You?'

The gate opened a fraction, and Herta slipped inside.

'I'm sorry. Something's happened.'

They sat in the same kitchen, at the same table we did when we paid Lilo a visit and she would ask me what I'd like. 'A hot choc-olate, Fips?' They had treats like that there. It was a large room with a fairly low ceiling and a flight of stairs leading down to the workshop, which was dark that evening.

If Lilo wasn't already in on their escape plans, then Herta had to make her privy to them now. She had to reveal Georg's trip to Bonn and the letter that had arrived that morning, which explained why they hadn't come to the pub with the other guests after the funeral for coffee and cake.

Despite her own need for consolation, Lilo listened. Then she looked up and said, 'What now?'

Herta shrugged her shoulders. It was too late. Too late for anything. They had made no preparations. They would have to leave the furniture, the carpets, the pictures, the china and everything else behind. The only thing they might still be able to do was withdraw their savings. But what then? What could you do with them? It wasn't worth anything in the West. What held its value? Jewellery? Gold? Of course. But what if you had neither of those things, only a few hundred marks?

'How much do you have?' Lilo asked.

'Six hundred,' Herta replied.

'Six hundred?'

'Maybe a little more.'

Lilo had a think. 'A camera,' she said after a few seconds.

'A camera?' Herta asked. 'Where would I get one?'

Lilo laid her hand on her friend's arm and said, 'Leave it to me. I'll take care of it.'

When they had talked everything through, Lilo accompanied Herta back out into the yard but instead of turning back, she walked with her for a while. She followed Herta out of the gate into the street and linked arms with her, and they went along Brandenburgerstrasse, keeping close to the houses. Almost like old times when, as little girls, the two of them had roamed the streets, imagining their future life in Berlin.

The streetlamps had gone out, the moon appeared between the rushing clouds, bathing everything in a leaden light, and the cobbles were still dappled from the rain, the tail end of the heavier downpour that Georg, locked in the toilet, heard beating on the train roof as it rolled towards Potsdam.

At the foot of the bridge Lilo hugged Herta and said one last time, 'I'll take care of it', already knocking on Heinze's door in her thoughts, and then she turned back while Herta climbed up the sloping bridge. She stopped at the top and took a deep breath. The air was cool. Rainy air. Below her the glittering ribbon of the canal and beyond it, framed by trees, the lawn in the park: the site of her first dream.

There were three photo shops in Plothow that also sold cameras. People called them photo workshops, although the workshops were actually small rooms behind the stores. Saalmann, Heinze and Wille were the owners' names. Did they already have televisions? Or had they (at least one of them) ordered a set, a Rubens or a Rembrandt that wasn't going to be delivered for ages as they were too far down the waiting list?

This was what Lilo was thinking about. Her grounds for optimism. After walking down Mühlenstrasse, she turned right into Magdeburgerstrasse where Heinze lived. His was the name that had occurred to her as she went through the list mentally. It was way past ten. So what? They were acquainted.

The first-floor windows are brightly lit, but below, on the ground floor where Heinze lives, the shutters are closed. She knocks. He opens them a tiny crack. Oh, it's you. Can I come in? Sure. She's in mourning, having just lost her husband, but that will not have been a factor in the deal she proposes, which he accepts.

'Hmm,' he said after Lilo had presented the situation, naming no names. 'An Exakta Varex would be best.'

They were sitting in the living room. He flicked through the lists he had fetched from the shop.

A Cyclopean 35 mm single-lens reflex camera with an f2.8 Zeiss Tessar 50 mm lens and aperture priority, a recent model equipped with three flash sockets.

Lilo nodded. Yes, we'll take it.

However, Heinze couldn't simply go into the shop and take it off the shelf. This camera needed ordering too. This one most definitely.

Whatever. Maybe luck came to their rescue, maybe Heinze pulled out all the stops in return for moving to the top of the waiting list for a Rembrandt television set. Whatever happened, Herta had the camera when we boarded the train three days later. She had a large suitcase, a bag, the book of legends from the Harz region which she read to the boy as they travelled towards the border. And at the bottom of the suitcase, among the underwear, was the camera.

After they moved into the flat in Heubachstrasse, it was kept in the bedroom wardrobe with all their other valuables.

*

The cycle tour to Brandenburg in December '91? They were still alive. Yes, December; not the first trip but the first time since Herta's move back to Tautenburg had encouraged me to set out on her trail. I departed in early December and returned in mid-December, on such a stormy day that the taxi driver who drove me home refused to get out of the car.

'Enough to blow your hat off,' he said, and he was indeed wearing one, a leather narrow-brimmed hat perched on the back of his head like a carnival cap. He pocketed the fare and clasped the wheel with both hands.

'The boot's open,' he said, staring out at the street so I would realize I was out of luck. I got out, walked round the car, opened the boot and took out my suitcase.

So much snow had fallen in East Germany in the previous three days that the short distance from Potsdam to Plothow, normally a 45-minute drive, took three hours. It was the kind of sudden, early cold snap no one had seen for years.

It had already begun to thaw by the time I travelled back to Frankfurt, but the snow was still deep, ploughed into walls along the sides of the roads, and the fields through which the train rolled were covered with snow; then the blanket of snow thinned out after Magdeburg and on the other side of Helmstedt it was gone, as if the old border now marked the dividing line between two climatic zones. A grey country appeared, washed uniformly clean by rain. And when I got off the train it was as warm as springtime; what remained was the wind, a wind that kept reviving itself, inter- mittently whipping itself into a storm and sending hats flying through the air.

That was in December, and in January I began going for strolls, as advised by a doctor I consulted about precordial anxiety.

I walked the same streets he had walked through with Mila. The estate: a mishmash of detached and semi-detached houses built in the sixties and seventies, with roads named Danzig Street or East Prussia Embankment, home to tradesmen and employees, and although it was not an upmarket area, I was struck by the signs of prosperity everywhere. It seemed as if the houses were more solidly built than in Plothow, on firmer and more stable foundations, and I thought that even the layout of the gardens under the grey, rain- flecked light corresponded to an underlying plan.

GERT LOSCHÜTZ

Yet it was precisely this aspect that soon began to bore me, and so I headed out into the marsh, up the orchard-covered slope and a little way along the middle path leading through the fields and down into the woods. However, even the landscape seemed so tidy that I no longer enjoyed looking at it. I had returned to a symmetrical world, which the other side was doing its best to emulate. All over East Germany you would see construction machinery tearing up the ground and houses being replastered, and teams of surveyors roamed the outskirts of towns, erecting signs saying what was going to be built there: a sewage treatment plant, a hospital, a shopping centre. It was the same in Berlin, Potsdam and Plothow.

Roads were levelled, fire breaks many metres wide cut through the forests, potholes filled, level crossings fitted with barriers or at least traffic lights, the ruined production facilities of bankrupt companies demolished, blocks of flats, indeed entire streets and neighbourhoods renovated, buildings reroofed, busted doors and windows replaced . . .

8

Plothow was a farming town whose more village-like part, the bit I knew best, was made up of single-storey or, at most, two-storey brick houses with gardens. Originally a farming village, it was clustered around two centres: the former manor house with its grounds and the streets radiating out from it; and the church overgrown with lilac bushes and crippled locust trees. The latter boasted most of the two-storey houses, the school, the farmers' houses and the houses of the canal men who were often away on their barges for weeks at a time.

Tautenburg, on the other hand, was a slate town. They had settled in a slate-mining region. Turning off the motorway, you drove past the slate quarries, large stone-scattered expanses nestling inside hairpin bends, and glimpsed for a second the pile drivers used to break the stone out of the ground, the towering conveyor belts and the trucks—grey monsters that would suddenly appear around a corner, like envoys from the world of slate, forcing other vehicles to mount the verge so they could pass.

Divided by a small water course lined with grey stone, the town itself lies between two hills or, more accurately, between the foothills of two ranges of low mountains. On one side, as if to indicate a linguistic border, the Westerwald ends, and on the other side the Rothaargebirge begins. The linguistic distinction primarily took the form of a tiny vowel shift that no outsider could detect but which indicated to locals which part of town you were from.

In general, though, it was a dialect full of guttural 'r's, spoken as if the tongue was paralysed deep in the throat, and it was impenetrable to foreigners.

The houses were clad with slate and roofed with slate, and the streets in the old town were so narrow that it had been possible to rip out whole rows of houses in the seventies without creating a hole in the town centre. On the very spot where the castle stood before its destruction in the Seven Years' War, a tower reminiscent of a medieval fortress looms over the town like a raised finger, the first thing you see as you approach by train and the last sight as you depart, and a little below it is the town church, built of the same grey stone, the burial place, until the first half of the eighteenth century, of the counts of Nassau, who once resided in the castle.

Strolling around between the tower and the church at the top, you have a view down into the valleys. Left and right of the roads, which were used mainly by tractors with their trailers in the late fifties when we moved there, the land is now occupied by industry—the enamel works, the brickworks and the steelworks, next to them a series of smaller companies, their suppliers, hardware stores, garages and petrol stations; however, the grounds of the textile factory where Georg found a job after they arrived are hidden from sight. It is on the banks of the river Taute but obscured by the roofs of the old town.

What you can see is the lower part of Heubachstrasse—named after a stream that runs along the back of the houses before disappearing at its midpoint into a pipe through which it continues underground before joining the Taute near the Obertor bridge—and the building containing their first and last flat they shared in the West. Outside the raised front door stood a wrought-iron fountain, a sort of trough into which a thin jet of water gushed from a lion's head attached to the end of a rusty pipe. This was where the children met in the afternoon when they had finished their homework.

The building had a name, the Tobacco Factory, although it isn't clear whether it had been a manufacturing site or had got the name because its occupants used to earn themselves a little extra income by processing tobacco in the evenings after their day jobs; in any case, the leaves were laid out to dry in the attic, then chopped up and packed into tins or rolled into cigars on the lower floors. It wasn't tobacco the house smelt of, though; it was mould.

Although the building was on a rise, the cellar exuded a foul smell that merged with the food odours from the flats in the summer and those from the loos on the landings to form a putrid stench, which is why my mother would fling the windows open whenever she went downstairs. Not that it helped, mind you; the stench remained. The stones, the beams, and the wattle of the walls were steeped in it.

Another house in the street was called 'The Drunken Man' because it leant against the next-door house like an alcoholic in need of support. A third one, the scene of a crime, was called 'The Pitchhole'. A man had doused his wife in petrol and set fire to her. Ulli, one of the boys I hung out with by the fountain in the afternoons, said that he had seen her run out into the street in flames. That couldn't be true, though, because another boy, Richard, knew that the incident had taken place at least 40 years ago. And a third boy said, 'Not 40, 140', and it wasn't petrol but pitch, hence the name.

But Richard tapped his forehead with his finger. 'Pitch? Don't be so stupid.'

He was a few years older than me, in his final year of primary school, and he lived on the same floor as us with his mother, a widow who had fled from the Sudetenland, carrying him in her arms. He had small, compact body (I remember it being as long as it was wide), red hair and light, almost white eyelashes.

*

The spring of '57 it was. Georg had found a job straight away.

It was a time when everyone was needed. A few years later, the news showed exhausted-looking men with dark five-o'clock shadows on their chins and cheeks getting out of trains and looking with bewilderment at bouquets proffered by politicians who had turned up to greet the 100,000th guest worker. They came from southern Italy and settled on the outskirts of cities where industries had sprung up, and then one day the first ones arrived in the slate town; at first they lived in the wooden huts by the copse, and after a while they moved into the street and building where Herta and Georg used to live.

That hadn't happened yet, but, as if heralding that migration, the Venezia ice cream parlour opened soon after Herta and Georg's arrival. It was on Oranienplatz, the slate town's central square, and run by an Italian family who returned to Italy in winter when ice-cream sales dried up and came back the next spring. The parlour with a long ice cream counter, tables and chairs was a knocked-through ground-floor apartment in an old half-timbered building, its back wall taken up entirely by a mirror with a shelf full of sparkling glasses in front of it; posters were plastered diagonally across the walls—the Rialto bridge, St Mark's Square; fragrances of vanilla and chocolate wafted out into the street.

In the evenings, when the boy was in bed, they would some-times flee their wretched home and stroll around town, window-shopping. Grundig and Philips television sets could be seen in the shops, and a blue lacquered sign marked *Rotary Club* was emblazoned over the entrance of the hotel; next to a photo shop with small cameras lying in the window hung a glass display case containing pictures of the shooting festival that could be ordered inside. And in Marktstrasse, which was a greater draw for Herta than any other street, the Herzog department store had opened the previous year with a fashion show; it offered clothes for all the family. The salesrooms occupied two whole floors, as they had at Parvus'. Herta would go right up to the window, cup her hand over her eyes and nod. Yes, she knew them. She was familiar with these cuts from when she went to West Berlin to stock up on fashion magazines.

They would take in all the sights, then amble past the grand archway of their boy's high school and down Wielandstrasse to the lower town gate. The air was thick with the malty odour from the two breweries that were still in production at the time, and from the courtyards backing onto the river Taute came the clinking of crates and bottles being unloaded from lorries. They would turn right in front of the palace and, reaching Oranienplatz, go into the Venezia. They would take a seat at one of the small marble tables and cast an eye over the menu. It was a bit like their very first meet-ings: everything was new again. Herta would reach across the table, and he would lay his hand on her arm.

Whenever possible, they sat by the window. Girls walked past in the street, skirts twirling, and young, suntanned lads cruised in cabriolets around the square, at the centre of which stood the memorial to those who had lost their lives in the First World War—an iron column, surrounded by chains, with the names of the dead engraved on it.

After a while they would grow uneasy. The boy. Georg signalled to the waiter and paid. They walked up the main street, quicker now, and when they reached their building, they would catch sight of the battered letterboxes behind the door from which envelopes containing department store catalogues poked in the mornings. The other residents ordered what they needed from mail-order firms, buying not just furniture and clothes but also food and tins of soup and frankfurters, canned fruit and vegetables. First the postman brought the catalogues, then, two weeks later, another deliveryman would arrive with the large packages.

They went upstairs and the first thing they did upon entering their flat was to check on the boy, who quickly switched off the light when he heard them in the hall. Easing the door open, they saw that he was asleep. At least that's how it appeared. In fact, he would only go to sleep when they got back and he heard their footsteps, their muted voices. His breathing would become deeper. After a while, practically as he dozed off, he would hear them sit down in the living room and talk quietly.

Is that right? Yes. Nothing suggested separation, nothing at all, and yet it had already begun. One of those harmless evenings, after they got back from the ice cream parlour, when she asked what they should do with the camera. Keep it? No. Sell it then. But how? Well, they'd have to go into a shop and offer to sell it. In the photo shop in the main street where they'd just been standing? For instance. Sure. He nodded.

9

In Plothow Georg would catch the train to work. It took him 20 minutes to Brandenburg, and if it was too late in the evening, Radinke, the driver, would drop him home. In the slate town, it was a five-minute walk. He would walk along the Heubach, turn left into the upper main street, cross the road just before the Obertor bridge and he was already in the industrial estate where the textile factory had its offices and warehouses.

He got on well with Greiner, the owner, but he wasn't happy in this job. The company was too small for him, and the textile trade wasn't his thing. The fact that he still accepted the position was probably down to Schwepp, an acquaintance from the steelworks. He came from Plaue, a small town near Brandenburg and, after escaping from the East, had moved to Siegen, a place close by. He would come over some evenings. He'd drive his Ford Taunus, the one with the globe on the roundel mounted above the front grill, over the Kalteiche, a hill between Siegen and Tautenburg, and up Heubachstrass, parking so close to the fountain that the kids who hung out there until nightfall would threaten to slash his tyres. They were angry that someone dared to intrude on their group. However, Schwepp would beckon to one and, with a handshake, promote him to chief car watchman, personally accountable to him. As a token of his trust in the child, he would leave the driver's door open. He explained the dashboard to the boy and pointed to the glove compartment. 'Nothing in there,' he said. 'You can get in behind the wheel if you like.' After that, Schwepp would climb the stairs and sit in the kitchen with Georg and Herta far into the night.

Herta was delighted to see him—for Georg's sake. In Schwepp's presence he seemed to forget the worries that plagued him. He reacted to a remark by Schwepp—the meaning of which was lost on anyone else (including Herta) because it was something to do with the steelworks—by bursting out laughing, which triggered a short exchange no one else could follow, punctuated by repeated salvos of laughter. These were their brief trips down memory lane, and the words they called out to each other were a code scattered with allusions and abbreviations whose purpose was to exclude others.

After escaping to the West a year before us, Schwepp had returned to his old job. He was the sort of dealer who trades in anything and everything, from office furniture to scrap metal, but in the East he had worked at the same plant as Georg. Next door, only separated from their site by a wire fence, was the base of a Russian armoured corps—no coincidence, they thought—and when they sat in the canteen and weren't sure if the man at the next table was to be trusted or not, they would resort to this jargon in which they were still so proficient that they could reach for it when necessary, and they would joke around until they realized from the growing silence that it was time to return to a language everyone understood.

'It's just to get started, Georg,' he will have said, before adding that the textile factory was a factory in name only.

A few years after the war, the current owner, the founder's grandson, had decided to cease production while on a trip to England. He'd fallen in love with the British lifestyle—English tea, bacon and eggs and the English sense of fair play, which he regarded, along with humour, as a cornerstone of the democratic system. The sign on the arch above the entrance to the site on the banks of the Taute, with its large one-story halls, the Greiners' house and the gazebo, still said Greiner's Textile Factory, but the fabrics were imported now. They arrived from England in man-sized bales and were unloaded from the truck and transferred into the halls where the looms had once stood.

'Tweed', Greiner said one evening after he had caught sight of me roaming around the site.

I would occasionally do this when I picked my father up from work. I'd wait at the entrance or, if this went on for too long, go to the Greiners' villa which stood in a garden behind the yard. I would unlatch the gate and walk up the flagstone path past the flowerbeds to the house from which a pergola led to a gazebo over-looking the Taute.

'Take note, Philipp. There is nothing in the whole wide world to rival tweed.'

It was impossible to pronounce my name in a more English fashion than he did, clipping Philipp so short that it sounded like Flip. I can remember that and also what he was wearing that day, a sand-coloured three-piece suit, and his shoes were brown too, made of shagreen leather with a hole pattern around the edge. Another thing I remember was his car. Yes, that above all else—a grey Bentley with a wooden dashboard that, in a certain light, glowed a warm, transparent yellow like amber. Inside, it was so high that the only time I rode in it I could stand up without my head touching the fabric on the inside of the roof—the sky. The steering wheel was on the right, which often startled me when I spotted the car on the road because I would automatically look at the empty left seat; but it was often too late by the time I looked to the right, and I was therefore unable to tell who'd been at the wheel, Greiner or Kriwett, the chauffeur who was the only other person his boss allowed to drive it.

People called Greiner 'the boss', or 'Jochen'.

Yes, they used his first name too, though not to his face, not so that Greiner could hear it, but whenever he wasn't around people would refer to Jochen. They had known him since he was a boy and now he was grown up, they stuck to his first name whenever he was mentioned in conversation.

Greiner had this box-shaped car and Lisa, his wife, had a Mini with a Union Jack sticker next to the rear light. I sometimes saw it parked in the yard, where two lads washed it and the Bentley and rubbed the two cars dry. Kriwett would generally be leaning against a nearby wall, keeping an eye on them, and once when I came past and he recognized me, he said, 'That's Frau Lisa's car.' Disparagingly, because it was so small.

Frau Greiner came outside just then. A red scarf draped around her neck, she stepped out of the office wing and tottered down the few steps, causing Kriwett to takes his hands out of his pockets and call, 'The little car will only be a minute or so.' She, however, walked away towards the town without looking up, probably without even hearing him. Kriwett watched her go until, reduced to a swaying red dot, she went up the rise to the yard entrance and crossed the road to the main street on the other side.

He, Kriwett, also pronounced a strange 'r', not a gurgling one like people in Tautenburg nor Greiner's English one, but the Baltic 'r', which sounded like a trill. He came from Riga and lived with his family in an annex of the villa, for he was caretaker as well as chauffeur. He usually wore a peaked cap, pulled down so far that his eyes were in shadow.

I knew one of the boys Kriwett chose to wash the car. Axel was one of Greiner's warehouse workers; in the evenings he used to stand around smoking with Richard by the foundation. Richard was a boxer, he was in the club, and I initially thought Axel was too, another boxer, but then I saw he had a crippled left arm. He couldn't bend it properly and so—if he held his cigarette in this hand—he didn't bring the cigarette to his mouth but his mouth to the cigarette, which made him look like a bird dipping its beak in a birdbath. He was a head taller than Richard, his face was all spotty, and since he had often seen me in the yard, he told me that Kriwett was a member of the Schlaraffia society where he was known as the 'Lion of the Eastern Seas', whereas Greiner, who belonged to the same society, was called 'Lord Clifden' after a place in Ireland where an especially hard-wearing tweed was woven.

'Rubbish,' my father said when I told him this, but we saw the two of them, Kriwett and Greiner, a few days later. It must have been a Sunday afternoon, coffee time. After going for a walk on the hill near the castle, we went into the restaurant in the middle of the main street, the one with the blue *Rotary Club* sign, and sat down by the window, he at one end of the table with his back to the wall, and my mother and I opposite each other on the long sides.

The waitress walked across the restaurant, balancing a tray, and pushed down the handle of the door into the side room, a function room, with her elbow. As the door swung back, I saw my father's eyes narrow and the corners of his mouth begin to twitch and, glancing round, I caught sight of Kriwett through the open door.

Decked out in a green waistcoat with protruding puff sleeves, Kriwett was sitting on a raised dais at the end of the room with a heavy chain around his neck, and in front of him sat people in mediaeval dress, looking up at him from two rows of tables that had been pushed together. One of them was Greiner; he had a green cap on his head with a thin, quivering feather in it. From the wall behind Kriwett hung a banner with the words *In arte voluptas* on it. The waitress handed him a glass over the table and as Greiner leant forward to take it from her, he spotted us, raised his hand in greeting and waved. My father nodded, and again I saw the same twitching at the corners of his lips as if he were desperately stifling a laugh.

'What is it?' asked my mother, who hadn't seen anything, but he just shook his head slightly and gave me a sharp look.

There were three photo shops in the slate town too, two on the main street and one at the beginning of Solmsstrasse, whose buildings, like the stud farm, had been constructed with stone from the ruined castle. Most of the local council offices were there.

Georg was not a salesman. He didn't like acting the supplicant, which is what he felt like when he had to negotiate with the shopkeepers. He would set out in the evenings when he got back from Greiner's. Every second or third evening. He only had time in the evenings. He worked by day and every second or third day he would come home early, open his bag, unpack his lunchbox, put the camera in the bag and shut it again. Every movement was distinct, as if he had weights hanging from his arms. I would sit on the kitchen bench and observe him, and if he noticed me watching, he would nod.

'So, are we off?'

First, he paid a visit to the photo shops in Tautenburg, but none of them showed any interest. Next, he went to the nearby towns, to Siegen where Schwepp lived, and then in the other direction, to Wetzlar. And every time he stepped into a shop, he had to utter the same stupid words: 'I have a camera here.' It was stupid because they could clearly see that he had one. He went inside, placed it on the counter and said, 'I have a camera here. Do you think you might be interested?'

'Let's have a look. Is it new?'

'Brand new.'

'Can I see the receipt?'

'I don't have it any more.'

'And the box?'

'What box?'

'The packaging. It must have come in some kind of packaging.'

As if Herta had nothing better to do than lug a box over the border.

They would size him up and size the camera up and then make him an offer so ridiculously low that he would put it back in the bag and leave. The next day or the day after that, he would start all over again.

'If only I hadn't brought the thing with me,' Herta said when he got home.

To which he replied, 'No, it was the right thing to do.'

'It was a hare-brained idea.'

It had long since ceased to be about the money and more about proving to her that she'd been right.

She'd be on the lookout for him. After he had set down the bag on the chair without a word, she would get up, go over to the bag, open it, remove the camera, take it into the bedroom and put it back in the wardrobe. It went on like this for half the summer until one evening he came home and announced from the doorway that he had managed to sell it.

Yes, it's a summer's evening, the window is open, light slanting in. It's the only window, which is why there's not much light. It doesn't illuminate the kitchen properly. Some of the corners are always dark. Even on really bright days, some parts are in shadow. The cries of the children standing around the fountain or sitting on the railing in front of the house drift up, a rising and falling tide of cries, like the calls of birds flying away and then circling closer again.

She's standing at the sink, having just cleared away the dishes and deposited them there. She tenses and turns around when she hears him come in.

'The camera?' she asks.

She stares at him in such disbelief that he nods. Against all the odds he nods vigorously. He's standing by the door, in a white shirt that glows in that dark corner; she's standing at the sink whereas I'm sitting on the kitchen bench. The dull square of light on the floor.

He finally breaks away from the corner, walks over and counts out four banknotes onto the table, as if in evidence. She wipes her hands on her hips, comes over to join him and stares at the money.

That is the image.

It was a Friday, yes a Friday evening, and two days later there was a knock on the door, a banging on the cracked wooden door, and at the same time the twist doorbell rang so insistently and piercingly that it startled me in my room on the other side of the flat. I'd been awake but dozing.

It wasn't so early, about half past eight. I could see from the lines I'd drawn with a pencil on the window cross, which allowed me to tell the time—the higher the sun rose, the farther down the window the shadow moved. The long lines marked a full hour, the short ones half an hour.

Voices and footsteps outside, creaking floorboards. I got up, opened the living room door and peered out into the short passageway leading to the kitchen. My father was sitting at the table with two men. He was still in his pyjamas whereas the other two were dressed, one in uniform, the other in a suit; it might have been this disparity that made him appear so defenceless. The baggy pyjama bottoms, his bare feet in the open slippers. He asked if he was allowed to get dressed. 'Of course.' They nodded.

Herta was standing at the window, her hand on the brass knob. The suited man turned to her and said he was sorry but they would have to take him with them, to which she also nodded, without apparently taking in the import of these words. She was wearing a striped man's dressing gown; the outsized sleeves were rolled up, and the top of her nightgown was peeking out above the rolled collar.

He went into the bedroom, with the uniformed man close behind. After a short while they returned, he now dressed, and all three went down the stairs, first the man in the suit, then him and the uniformed man last.

I remember because he offered to let the two men go ahead, raising one hand in the doorway to signal that they should please go first. There was no question of this happening, however—they made him walk between them. He ducked as he passed through the doorway so as not to bang his head on the lintel (a reflex since he was young, so he didn't have to think about it), whereas the other two didn't need to duck. Immediately afterwards, they could be heard clattering down the stairs.

And I remember another thing: his humming. He was humming as he went out of the door. His mouth was shut, but he was humming a song or some kind of tune. This humming enveloped him like a shell; you would hear it sometimes, when he was extremely tense, maybe less of a humming than a vibration, something that appeared to come from deep inside his chest, an irregular series of notes that only gradually coalesced into a melody. He would hum or whistle to himself to avoid losing face. It helped him to keep his composure; it soothed his agitation; it was a straw to cling to in his anxiety.

This humming was linked to his fear, but the two men who were leading him away obviously saw it as a particularly deplorable lack of respect, because their initially sympathetic expressions hardened. The further he retreated behind his wall of sound, the surlier they became, and when the clatter of feet in the staircase had died away and we looked out of the window, we saw them pushing him towards their car, a dark-blue VW parked next to the fountain, a spectacle that lured children out of the building and grown-ups to their windows on that quiet Sunday morning. Wasn't it time for church too? Yes, the hour of cream-coloured cardigans and white ankle socks and hands holding up songbooks for all to see; the churchgoers came trotting down Heubachstrasse, swung right a little beyond the fountain into the narrow lane that led up to the town church and turned their heads inquisitively at the sight of the police car.

The children stood around the fountain and the car, the adults leaned out of the windows and the churchgoers turned their heads, and so it could be said that every local resident with a window overlooking the scene and anyone who was already out and about witnessed his arrest.

They pushed or shoved him along and when they reached the car, the uniformed man opened the door and tilted the seat forward while the other man forced him into the back. He got in and, as he looked up once again at the window where we were standing, the man in civilian clothes pushed his head down. He shook off his hand and stood up straight again, so that it looked for a moment as if the two of them were wrestling, but then he gave in, climbed into the car and it immediately set off down the street—to applause from the bystanders, I feel like saying, but that wasn't how it was, or not only. As soon as things calmed down again, little Frau Wolf, Richard's mother, squeezed into our kitchen, sat down next to Herta and took her hand.

10

That evening, that Friday evening, my father had already been on his way to the railway station to travel to Giessen, the city on the other side of Wetzlar from Tautenburg, but then he turned back and went to the factory. The working day was long since over, but he had a key. In the two months he had been working for Greiner, Georg had become so indispensable to his boss that he not only had access to the offices but also to the safe in Greiner's office. He opened it and removed 320 marks, which was roughly the amount he ought to have got for the camera. That was how much Herta had paid for it in East German marks.

Greiner had flown to London that morning to meet a business friend, the man who supplied them with fabrics, and was planning to be back by Wednesday evening. The Monday was the first of July, the day salaries were deposited in employees' accounts; Georg intended to withdraw the money immediately and return to the safe the 320 marks he'd removed. That's not how things turned out, though. For whatever reason, Greiner hadn't travelled to London and had instead gone to the office on Saturday, as he sometimes did. He'd noticed the missing money and, given that the only other person who had a key to the safe was his employee Georg Karst, had reported the matter to the police.

This was what Georg told her when she was finally allowed to speak to him. He hadn't planned to steal the money, just borrow it.

The police station was in a wing of the town hall opposite the small footbridge over the Taute, but it was reached via the main entrance of the town hall. She crossed the echoing foyer with its noticeboards and partitions, went up three steps and stepped through the swing door into the corridor connecting the town hall to the wing and then sat opposite him at a brown wooden table in a small room whose barred window looked out over the Taute. Out of the corner of her eye she could see the grey stone wall along the stream. When she reached across the table to touch him and take his hand in hers, as she had done on their dates in Plothow, the police officer sitting by the door behind her intervened.

'Stop that, please,' he called, craning his neck.

She pulled back her hand and listened to Georg again. 'So everything's all right then,' she said.

Of course, he hadn't acted properly. Not completely properly. On the other hand, her husband hadn't intended to enrich himself or harm the company. Had Greiner gone away over the weekend as planned, he wouldn't have noticed a thing.

'You've got to talk to him,' she said. 'He'll see that you didn't mean to do anything wrong.'

But he shook his head. 'No,' he said. 'There's no point.'

'Why not?'

Now she heard the other version. Now he told her what everybody else was saying—Greiner, that is—whose views the others had made their own. The police, the public prosecutor, the investigating judge: they all believed Greiner's depiction of events, reporting not the comparatively small sum of 320 marks but 12,000.

'12,000?' she cried.

He looked away and nodded. '12,000. Yet there were at most—no, I counted the money: exactly—*exactly* 600 in the safe.'

'Did you tell the police?'

'Of course I did.'

'And?'

'Greiner's sticking to his story that 12,000 are missing.'

At this she had put her hands over her mouth because she could sense that sound in her throat again—the sound of sobbing.

The first days of July, just before the summer holidays, were so hot that damp that was still in the walls from the winter evaporated; the stone heated up and the dark grey turned a chalky hue like exuded salt; the Taute had almost dried up and so between the collapsed heaps of foam you could see large stones, their tops already dry, around which dead fish gathered, bright bellies up, as if looking for something to cling onto. And over it all hung the odour of decay the heat had released from the gullies and dark nooks.

When she entered the house with the fountain outside, she went up the staircase full of kitchen and toilet smells, and halfway up she must have thought that she now belonged here. She didn't like the town or the countryside but what she liked least of all was the building they lived in, the cramped conditions and the stench. Now, she thought, it had become her stench too. Wasn't it the case that shortly after they'd moved in, also on a Sunday morning, a police car had pulled up outside and they had heard a clattering of shoes, banging on a door, loud shouts—'Open up!'—because they had arrested a man living on the first floor who was accused of stealing a car, burglary and stabbing someone? That seemed nothing unusual here. Now they—she, her husband and her boy—belonged. They belonged with these people. Now they had arrived.

Hello, Tautenburg, here we are.

After relaying everything she thought she could tell me, she went into the living room, drew the curtains—the clatter of the rings with which they were attached to the rail—and then sat immobile in the armchair in the green-tinted light, feet still in her parallel shoes. She sat like that until evening without moving. It stayed light late, but eventually the bright green darkened to a deep bottle-green. Dusk fell, then darkness. I tiptoed down the passageway past the open door but I didn't dare to speak to her and ended up cutting myself a slice of bread in the kitchen and taking it to my room.

'Fips, Fips,' she called, 'you need to eat something.'

Apparently, she couldn't bring herself to eat anything or even to get up from her chair. At long last I saw the light in the corridor go on, heard the floorboards creak and saw her coming along the passageway in her stockings.

'Do you think you can put yourself to bed?'

I nodded. Of course. Why not?

'Good,' she said. 'You do that, OK?'

She took her coat off its hook and went to the door. Her shoes—pumps, I now know—were still dangling from the index finger and middle finger of her left hand. She dropped them on the floor, righted them with one foot and slipped them on. Before opening the door she glanced at the hall mirror, although not as she usually did when she went out, but with a kind of reflex, in the same perfunctory way as she had when setting out for the police station.

This was at about nine. It was 11 when she got back. I could tell from the dark dial of my watch. She'd been away for two hours. Hearing her footsteps on the stairs, I turned out the light that had been on the whole time and pretended to be asleep, at my side the book I had been trying but unable to read because the letters swam before my eyes. I longed for the distraction the story would bring, but no sooner had I opened it than everything began to blur.

'You're awake, Fips,' she said as she came in. She bent down and put her hand on my shoulder. 'Can you hear me?'

I kept breathing deeply in and out, though, and feeling a draught on my ear, I rolled over indignantly onto my tummy and put the pillow over my head. She ran her fingers along my back, turned away with a sigh and left the room. So it was the next day before I heard where she'd been. She had gone to confront Greiner and finding him out, had sat down on the steps and waited for his return. Eventually the car had pulled into the courtyard—not the Bentley but the Mini; he and his wife had gone out together.

She had walked up to him and said, 'I beg you, Herr Greiner.'

To which he immediately replied that he would see what he could do, but she must see why he had had to report the matter.

A few nights later, I was woken by the noise of the two halves of a window banging together. It was a warm summer night, and the wind was up as before a storm. I got out of bed, shut the window and went to the kitchen for a glass of water. The bedroom door was slightly ajar. Peering inside, I saw that the bed was still made. Herta wasn't at home. She couldn't have gone back to Plothow, I thought, because she didn't like anything there. She was the one who had been desperate to leave and, since she had left, longed to return. At least that's what I imagined. I turned on all the lamps, switched on every light in the entire flat and then sat down in one of the new armchairs; I think they were green. And then—I don't know how long I sat there; did I fall asleep?—I heard her footsteps on the stairs and the jangle of the key in the lock.

'What are you doing here?' she said as she came in. 'Why aren't you asleep? Come on, darling, go to bed. I only went out for a minute to get some fresh air.'

I stayed awake the next night and the one after that. Then, at about ten when it was almost dark, I heard noises in the kitchen and immediately afterwards the gentle click of the door. My clothes were lying on the chair. I got dressed, rushed down the stairs after her and ran past the fountain into the street. Yes, there she was. The click of her heels on the cobbles as she walked along close to the kerb, almost in the road while I stuck to the walls of the houses. She didn't have a suitcase, just a little bag that would barely hold a sandwich. A parcel, that's what it looked like—something square or cubic made the thin material bulge. You couldn't travel back across the border with that, and so I thought it would be better to keep an eye on her.

At the junction she turned left, which wasn't the way to the station but to the Obertor bridge and the Taute. That would have been the moment to turn back, but I carried on following her, across the road onto the premises of the textile factory which lay in shadow. She crossed the yard and pushed down the handle of the garden gate, beyond which lay the Greiner's house.

She wants to talk to him again, I thought. *She wants to tell him to withdraw his complaint.*

Strangely, though, she didn't take the flagstone path to the house but the gravel path that bypassed the house and led directly to the Taute and the gazebo overlooking it. She kept to the middle of the path whereas I crept across the lawn beside it so she wouldn't hear me. Half hidden by the trees and bushes, horse chestnuts and rhododendrons, I followed her.

That evening the curtains, which were generally open, were closed; thick yellow curtains through which seeped a dim light you could only see if you approached to within a few metres of the gazebo. Only then could you make out the honey-coloured light for which she headed without the slightest hesitation. I heard her knock three times in quick succession and saw the door open. I got a brief glimpse of Greiner before it shut again. I sat down on the grass with my back against a tree and waited. It wouldn't be long before she reappeared. When I got bored of this, I stood up and went over to listen to what they were saying, but even though the walls were only made of planks dovetailed together, I couldn't hear a sound, not a word, and despite the low windows, the curtains prevented me from seeing anything. I walked around the octagonal gazebo—and then I saw.

The curtain on the window looking out over the Taute was drawn too, but there was a minute gap through which it was possible to peer into the room. There was only one room; the whole gazebo consisted of a single room furnished with old objects that might once have stood in the house but had been carried over here: a few leather chairs, a chest of drawers and, along the wall I was looking at, a sofa which they were sitting on, that is to say: she was sitting on it while he knelt in front of her with his head between her slightly parted legs, her dress pushed up above her stomach and her eyes closed.

There are two versions of what happened next and although I was involved, I couldn't vouch for the truth of one version over the other. Or maybe both were in fact made up.

One is that I smashed the glass with a stone and, climbing through the window, injured my arm (the scar is visible to this day); apparently I didn't even make it into the room because the sash bars blocked my path. According to the other, I jumped inside after shattering the pane and, still clasping the stone, threw myself at Greiner, who was only able to fend me off by wrestling me to the floor on top of the scattered glass shards; I tried to cushion my fall with my hands, but they hit the glass first.

The only certainty is that the wound, a cut to my lower arm, bled so copiously that my shirt and trousers, Herta's dress, the floor, the sofa and Greiner's suit were spattered with blood as it spurted like a fountain from the damaged vein until Greiner eventually found the right spot to press, a hand's breadth above the cut.

'To hospital,' he said. 'I'll take him to hospital. You stay here.'

'No,' she said, 'I'm coming too.'

I stood between her legs in the back as he drove. She was clasping my arm hard with both hands, but as soon as she loosened her grip, the blood began to drip onto her dress, which she had buttoned up lopsidedly in her haste. As we drove through town to the hospital, over the Taute and the railway tracks, uphill through the newly developed area, I saw the button in the wrong hole, bunching the material over her chest, creating two ugly folds and making the fabric stand out from her neck.

Greiner was in front, at the wheel. From time to time he would turn round and say, 'He ought to lie down.'

I couldn't see it, but I could tell from the sound of his voice when he glanced round. Or was Kriwett driving?

Yes, Kriwett was there too. It was he who had fetched the car from the garage and spread out a blanket on the floor while the others, Herta and Greiner, tried to staunch the bleeding. In the meantime, out in the yard, they had got hold of a belt and wrapped it around my upper arm, but it didn't work, however tightly they pulled, and the blood continued to flow; the surest method was for them to press down with their thumb on a particular spot on my arm.

'What on earth are you doing?' Herta whispered. With no free hand to embrace me, she did so by clamping my hips between her legs.

That was all, those few words. It was the only thing she said after the brief consultation with Greiner in the gazebo. *What on earth are you doing?* Then she stared straight ahead again in silence. Later at the hospital too, it was Greiner who spoke. The doctor came along the corridor, white coat flying, and bent over me while Greiner stood over him and whispered in his ear. He explained something, the doctor nodded and pushed Herta and me into the treatment room. I turned in the doorway and saw Kriwett again as he came in, cap in hand, and behind him, directly outside the entrance, the Bentley he had parked on the ramp so that Greiner could get straight in when he left.

*

On the last day before the summer holidays, Georg was waiting for me outside school. Unlike the mothers and fathers who had come to collect their children, he was not standing on the other side of the arch that divided the playground from the road but on the other side of the street. One of the two breweries had set up a bottling plant there in a flat-roofed building with a plate-glass front, giving a view of the conveyor belt with green lemonade bottles on it.

He had removed his jacket and draped it over his arm. He hesitated when he caught sight of me as if unsure whether I minded him picking me up. But when I ran towards him, he came alive and came to meet me.

'So,' he said, 'fancy an ice cream?'

'Are you back?'

He nodded and put his hand on my shoulder. We went along Marktstrasse and, after turning into the main street, sat down at one of the tables under parasols outside the Venezia ice-cream parlour. He'd been released that morning and come straight to Tautenburg. It had been almost a week since my accident, as Herta referred to my eruption into the gazebo, and I had grown used to calling it that too. They had changed the bandage twice. Both times I had climbed the hill with Herta and both times I had heard that it was healing nicely and that the wound would leave only a small scar.

'Does it still hurt?' he asked.

I shook my head.

Seemingly embarrassed, he looked away before clearing his throat and saying, 'That's not on.'

'What isn't?'

'Following someone.' He said it so quietly that I wasn't sure if I'd understood properly, but then he repeated it. 'Following someone. Fips,' he continued, 'Fips . . . I'm going to live somewhere else for a while.'

It was only then that I noticed that he had a bag with him, not the one he had carried down the stairs when he was arrested but a different, larger one next to his chair.

'For a while?'

'Yes. I'll be in touch.'

Later, much later, when I asked him to tell me about the circumstances of their breakup, I learnt that the jailer had come into his cell that morning after breakfast had been brought and instructed him to pack his things. He had led him to the prison director's office where he was informed that the warrant for his arrest had been overturned and he was free to leave the prison. When he asked why, the director had no answer; all he could say was that the charges had been dropped because the grounds for the arrest had been invalid. Apparently, he added as he flicked through his papers, the missing money, the 12,000, had reappeared.

I visited this same prison in the early seventies for one of my first reports for the Sunday supplement of a major newspaper. I photographed the yard, the workshops, the corridors, the cell wing and the cells themselves. I'd chosen that institution because it was one of the largest in Hessen, but that wasn't the only reason. Above all, it was his prison. He'd served time there. I wanted to see where he had been held, the little town in the Wetterau area, the old brick building with barred windows.

The director showed me around, and when I noticed the wire netting stretched like a life net over the space between the cell galleries, I thought of how he would have looked at this net every time he walked past . . . and that it would have reminded him that it was possible and if it wasn't possible in that way, you'd have to try another—you could tear off a strip of material from a bedsheet, roll it into a rope and tie it to the radiator, use a razorblade or put a plastic bag over your head. He hadn't, though. He had resisted the temptation.

11

In Plothow Herta would sometimes send me off with the thermos flask to the HO shop for ice cream in summer. For lunch she would cook rice pudding, sprinkled with sugar and cinnamon, or semolina with homemade raspberry syrup poured over it, and when I nagged her to go swimming, she would roll up two large towels and put them in the red net bag, and we would walk along to the old canal that branched off the new one a little beyond the park only to rejoin it about one and a half kilometres farther on.

One swimming spot was behind the bridge on the island between the new and old canals. We would go down the steps to the towpath, which was lined with poplars and, a little way along, choked with undergrowth. Horses and cows stood in the nearby fields off to the left, and to the right, beyond the canal, you could see the gardens and backs of the houses in Seedorferstrasse, their roofs so low that very few peeped above the fruit trees, the sole exception being the church tower, which was visible from the towpath, rising broad and grave over the trees and the roofs from its raised site in the middle of the small square behind the Seedorferstrasse.

There was a wide bed of reeds along the bank, leaving the water accessible in only a few spots. If you advanced into the canal, you were soon in deep, with your feet on something slippery or a root that was protruding from the bottom, and the water itself was so black that it was impossible to see anything, so that someone standing there up to their waist looked like a torso; as if they'd been sawn in half.

Herta would spread out the towels in the shade of a tree and dig out something to read while I glanced around to see if there was a boy I knew. From time to time, a horse-drawn cart would rumble over the bridge, and fine sand would trickle through the gaps between the logs, glinting in the sun's slanting rays like a swarm of gnats. In late afternoon, the older boys who had left school and were doing an apprenticeship with a tradesman would arrive. They propped their bikes against the masonry of the bridge, ran down to the canal, splashed some water on their faces and under their armpits, charged back up the bank, climbed onto the iron railing and leapt into the water—even though this was actually banned due to the risk of injury from assorted junk on the bottom of the canal—performing all kinds of mid-air tricks.

The other spot near the turn-off to the new canal was for adults only, which in mid-week meant mothers. They came here with the smaller kids to avoid the hubbub by the bridge over to the island, which is why we regularly argued in the last two years in Plothow when Herta wanted to go to the Bend (which is what this spot was called). I wasn't allowed into the water on my own, and why would I be interested in the little kids who might not even have been of school age yet? They couldn't be called playmates.

Sometimes Lilo would turn up out of the blue. If she didn't find us at home, she would guess that we'd gone swimming and make a detour to the canal to look for us instead of going back to town frustrated. She would cycle up, sit down on the towel next to Herta and unpack the slices of cake or watermelon she'd brought along. Afterwards, the two of them would recline, propping themselves up on their elbows, and chat quietly, often for the rest of the afternoon, occasionally gazing out at the barges plying their way along the new canal to Parey where they would pass through the lock onto the Elbe.

There were three routes to the slate town's swimming pool, the shortest of which crossed the textile factory grounds. You went past the warehouses and squeezed through a gap in the mesh fence at the back of the yard onto an old sports field, which hosted local school competitions but otherwise only served as a training ground for the football club's youth team. Here, if the wind was against you, your nose would catch the smell of chlorine from the open-air pool. Inaugurated the year before we arrived, it had a 50-metre competition pool, and a few apple trees still remained from the former orchards, although the children stripped them of their fruit long before it was ripe.

As I said, that was the shortest route. I'd taken it before Georg's arrest and a few times afterwards. After the incident, however, I gave the textile factory a wide berth, walking along the Taute before crossing a specially built footbridge to the pool.

I would put on my trunks in the general changing rooms, hang my things on the hanger, hand it in at the counter and cross the lawn to the fence where I would spread out the towel Herta had put in my rucksack, always in the same place (because I'd once seen Richard lie there?).

I lay down on my tummy, my chin on my hands, and closed my eyes. It was early still and so peaceful that you could hear the bees buzzing as they gathered nectar from the clover flowers among the grass, and the approaching and receding drone of cars on the main road to Haiger or on via Kalteiche to Siegen, or coming from that direction.

Later, as the pool filled up, the many individual sounds would merge into a composite wall of noise, a reverberating cacophonous bubble around the pool and the lawn, punctuated by the crack and whip of the three-metre board from the diving pool, followed by the sound of the diver piercing the surface, an incidental plop drawing your attention to the body arcing down sleekly into the depths, or a full-spectrum flop or a cannonballer's splash, followed by the patter of drops. Intermittently came an ear-splitting, explosive crackle of loudspeakers that usually preceded some instructions from the lifeguard or an announcement that a child had become separated from its parents.

The water in the old canal was so clogged with organic residue that you literally couldn't see your hand in front of your face when you dived in. Here in the slate town, on the other hand, it was so clear that you could see from one end of the shallow pool to the other. You could find your way underwater, which is how I got into div-ing, making good speed by doing proper breast-stroke arms and legs and spending almost more time under water than above it that summer. I had eyes like a rabbit's when I got home in the evening. The skin on my back, my shoulders and the backs of my knees was burnt and peeled after a few days; I slept on my tummy, covered only with a sheet; the back of my neck stung, but the next morning I would run off again down Heubachstrasse, over the Obertor bridge and along the Taute to the swimming pool.

'Be back by lunch,' Herta said, but there was an uncertainty in her voice which suggested to me that lunch could mean after-noon and afternoon, evening. I ate the sandwiches she gave me and when I got home in the evening and opened the door (I had a key now) I would see her in the kitchen at the sewing machine—her greatest wish; his gift—which had been one of the first things she'd bought in the slate town, and next to it patterns or, on a pulled-up chair, a fashion magazine with pictures she would refer to from time to time.

'Oh Fips,' she would say, looking up and casting an eye at the clock. 'This is no good, Fips. I said lunch. Aren't you hungry?'

She hardly ever went out any more, as far as I knew, only to the baker's or the corner shop. Frau Wolf would drop by in the evenings after work, and I realized, as she unhooked her dress and I was sent out, that Herta was sewing mainly for her.

Had three days passed, four, a week, when Georg came home? I climbed up the stairs, opened the door and spotted his bag by the wash basin. She obvious hadn't been expecting him because her sewing was strewn all over the place; the table, the chairs and the corner bench were all occupied, and so finding nowhere to sit, he had leant his shoulder against the window cross while she sat at the machine—stayed sitting at the machine, just as he had found her. They had clearly been deep in conversation because when I suddenly appeared, they stared at me in shock, as if I'd caught them red-handed. He recovered his composure, took a few steps towards me and gave me a hug. I felt his breath on my ear and neck. He'd been drinking—not much, but enough for me to smell it.

'Hey, Fips, how are you doing?'

I nodded and went along the short passageway to the living room, which was this side of my bedroom. That evening, when I was already in bed, I heard a kerfuffle next door, furniture being moved around, and when I got up again to take a look, I saw that he'd opened the sofa and was stretched out on it. He was lying on his back with his hand on his forehead. My noise made him look round.

'You're not asleep yet,' he said.

'It's the holidays.'

The sofa, both armchairs and the adjustable coffee table all smelt new. Of material, wood, varnish and glue, just like in a furniture store.

'Can I leave the door open?'

'Sure,' he replied, turning onto his side so he could see me. After a while he got up, turned off the ceiling lamp, came into my room, stood by the window and gazed out, the glow of the streetlights on his face.

'What's this?' he said.

I had wrapped some string around the window handle and threaded one end of it through the bottom of an empty tin can which I used as a mouthpiece and receiver. The string then ran across the street to a room above the corner shop where a boy from my school lived. We would sometimes play at telephoning, even though we weren't really friends. He would pick up the can and hold it to his ear.

'And?' he asked. 'Does it work?'

The next morning Herta came in, already dressed. She walked across the living room, past his empty sofa bed, stepped into my room, looked at me and went out again. And when I got up, I saw as I passed their bedroom, that the wardrobe doors were open. She had pulled over a chair and climbed onto it to fish down the suitcase and toss it on the bed.

'What's going on?' I asked.

'Oh Fips,' she said, 'these things happen.'

Her, scurrying around with her head down so that I had to jump out of the way if I didn't want to be mowed down; Georg, looking talked out, sitting with slumped shoulders in his shirt and trousers at the set kitchen table; the quick hug she gave me before picking up the suitcase; her brisk steps on the staircase . . .

Thinking back, I note that their separation, which caused me so much pain, took place almost without a sound. Something that prompted storms of emotion in others didn't even stir a breeze in them. That's the way it looked. He left and then came back; and when he got back, she left and moved to that room on the other side of the Taute. Some carrying of bags and suitcases back and forth, and it was done.

12

Richard's mother was a short, somewhat dumpy woman whose left knee had had to be put in a brace after a fall during her escape from the Sudetenland, so she dragged the leg as she walked and swayed from side to side. She still had the accent of her homeland. There was a large radiogram in her kitchen. On Saturday evenings a few invited guests from the second and third floors would come down to listen to the latest episode of the Durbridge crime series broadcast by Hessischer Rundfunk. Two long curly sausages were heated up on the gas stove, and she removed them from the water with a pair of wooden tongs, chopped them into large chunks and put them on a plate; they were served with slices of bread with lashings of butter and mustard from an open stone pot. The men drank beer they had brought along, and the women had a glass of Moselle wine.

Frau Wolf had a pretty face, and her greying hair was so well done that it looked as if she was about to go to a party.

On a commode next to the wireless stood a photo of her husband with a black ribbon in the top right-hand corner. He was dressed in his Wehrmacht uniform and had been killed by his Czech neighbours at home in Teplitz when the Red Army marched in. Richard, who had been two at the time, had witnessed it all and been struck dumb. He hadn't spoken a single word after that, not in Teplitz, not during their long escape, not after their arrival in the American zone, not at the kindergarten by the Taute which he went to after they arrived in the slate town, not at home in the flat where they still lived; only occasionally in his dreams had he emitted a gurgling sound that bubbled up from his throat until, one week before he started school, he suddenly opened his mouth and said he was hungry, causing Frau Wolf, who had just got home from work, to drop her bag in shock and start dancing around for joy on her stiff leg. Richard could talk completely normally. He knew all the words other children of his age knew, but had picked up the Tautenburger dialect during his five-year silence.

The radio play began at eight and ended around nine, during which time everyone listened attentively, leaning towards the radio with their heads slightly tilted and their arms propped on their knees. After the closing announcement, as they all sat upright once again, I put my plate in the sink, shook hands with Frau Wolf and crossed the landing to our flat where my father was sat over his correspondence or the green book in which he kept his records, while the others stayed on for a while and maybe even danced to music from the radio later.

Sometimes there would be a knock on the door shortly afterwards, and when I opened it, Richard would be there, asking if I wanted to come down to the front of the building with him. I turned to Georg who had overheard this invitation and looked up from his desk work.

'All right,' he said, 'you can go,' adding, 'But stay near the house!', to which Richard would call past me into the kitchen, 'We're only going to the fountain.'

Two or three times per week Richard could be seen running down the street with his boxing gloves around his neck. The way to training was already part of training, and sometimes, if I had time, I would join him and run alongside him to the gym where a square of fabric taped to the floor represented the ring. The majority of the session was spent skipping, lifting dumbbells and pummelling the sandbag, and later that year—or was it the next, after Herta's disappearance?—I went to the casino where the bouts were held: ABC Tautenburg versus BC Marburg, ABC versus BC Wetzlar.

The ring was erected in the large hall where balls and high school proms were held as well as the free-church congregation's missionary weekends. The spectators sat on folding benches, which were fetched out of a side room and set up around the ring half an hour before the contest. I helped out, so I got in free and would sit down in one of the back rows when the bouts started. Bernd and Werner came too, pushing their way along the row to me, and when everything was over, we would walk back through town, down the hill, over the tracks, a stretch along Friedrichstrasse, then over the stream via the Obertor bridge and, having reached the other side, uphill again.

Richard was small, broad-shouldered and muscular but not very fleet of foot. Featherweight, later lightweight and welter-weight: those were his categories. At the start of the fight he would stand there flat-footed in the ring, his legs slightly apart, his head between his raised shoulders and his arms flexed in readiness in front of his chest. Most opponents were a head taller than him, which meant that they only had to jab with their leading hand to keep him at bay. When he noticed them relying on this tactic, he would swat their hand and arm aside and take a few swings at their body, aiming to knock the wind out of them and force them to lower their guard, leaving their chin undefended. He wouldn't dodge his opponent's punches but sit in behind his double guard and allow them to rain down on his gloves and lower arms, waiting for the other kid to tire himself out before ducking under his arms and burrowing into him, fists pounding away like jackhammers.

After the fight, as he waited, hand in hand with the referee, for the result to be announced, he would shake himself like a wet dog that has just come out of the water and raise his left shoulder to his ear as he finally got to skip from one foot to the other. He wasn't bad: he won at least as many bouts as he lost.

Later, I now recall, he married a Vietnamese woman he'd met in Frankfurt and brought her to Tautenburg. Someone once made a lewd remark to her at the Saturday market, and he span round and floored the guy with a left hook.

13

Herta had found work straight away, even if it was of the kind she'd hoped to escape with Mill's help—a job at the Herzog three-floor clothes emporium. Her position was downstairs, however, in the ladies' department on the ground floor.

At lunchtime, on the way home from school, I would sometimes make a small detour to pass the shop and catch sight of her at one of the sales tables through the window. A touch of coolness and arrogance had entered her movements; her gestures were economical, and the way she studied the customers was icy. It's clear to me now what she thought: *On no account mistake me for one of you.* My reasons for consorting with one of your men exceeds the capacity of your tiny brains to grasp. And, by the way, I'm now returning him to you as below my standards.

People knew, of course, that she was the woman Greiner had been meeting. The news had spread like wildfire through the town, even reaching the ears of Richard, who looked up respectfully at me from under his blonde eyelashes and said, 'Goodness—with Greiner.' And the only person who could possibly have been to blame was Kriwett, the caretaker and chauffeur, who had come running at the sound of breaking glass. No one apart from him could have related the story. And now quite a few people came to the store merely for a glimpse of her. They generally turned up in twos or threes—two or three women would amble past the sales tables, casting glances to which Herta would try to respond with even icier glares.

Apparently thin-skinned despite her display of contempt, she simply turns on her heel and walks away when a lady, a villager with a big bun who has come into town to shop and knows nothing of Herta's affair, addresses her as 'Fräulein'.

'Now listen,' the head of department says after seeing the incident and walking after her, 'that's not on,' to which she reacts by rushing to her locker and fetching her coat, then, practically at the door, turns around and serves the lady as if nothing had happened.

The sewing machine—did she already have it then?

Yes, I can see her hunched over the kitchen table, in the corner of her mouth the pins she has removed from the material spooling away under the presser foot before sticking them in her sleeve a little above the elbow. That means that she had taken up sewing again, not, as in the canal town, with the heavy, foot-driven Singer but a portable machine, one of the first electric ones, which she had begged for when they moved to Tautenburg to help support the family and which then helped only to support her—and very little at that, because she only sold the clothes she sewed in exceptional circumstances; she tended to wear them herself. They served to distinguish herself from other women. Her memory for shapes was an advantage. She would examine a dress from every angle, memorizing its particularities, and could then replicate it; it was the same with clothes she saw pictured as full-page spreads in the fashion magazines lying around at the shop, evidence of a different and better world devoid of all ugliness, even though these items in the photos were on sale neither there nor anywhere else in town.

The articles on offer at the Herzog clothes store might be good enough for the others, but not for her. Taking the magazine pictures as her guide, she sewed her own dresses—mini-masterpieces, I know now, which were remarkable less for their extravagance than for their simplicity and the quality of the materials that sales representatives brought to the fabric department in their brown sample cases. Whenever one entered the store, she would meet him on the wide landing between the floors. He would open the large sample book and hold it up to the window while she ran her finger over the squares of cloth.

The shop closed at half past six. Having made no friends she needed to wait for to walk part of the way home, she was one of the first to leave. From her arm hung the bag containing the shopping she had done during the lunch break, hidden amongst it sometimes a purloined fashion magazine with those whole-page photos. By the time her colleagues stepped out of the shop's side entrance in twos and threes, she was usually halfway down the passageway leading to the main street. She walked quickly, without a sideways glance, crossed the footbridge spanning the stream in front of the town hall and, after leaving the town centre with its neon signs, plunged into the darkness of the street where she rented her room.

Georg usually got home around five. Yes, around five I would hear his footsteps on the stairs. He bounded up them two at a time, which is how I recognized that it was him and I checked that nothing was lying around—my school books, my tracksuit top, a glass I'd drunk from, the wrapping of a chocolate bar, a Jerry Cotton comic I'd borrowed from Richard.

Not that Georg would have told me off, but as soon as he spotted something lying around in the wrong place, he would tidy it away. He would put the glass in the sink, return the tracksuit top to my room and throw the chocolate wrapping in the bin. He wouldn't say anything, but the horror and fear that we might drown in the mess and chaos were plain on his face. This, I think, was his greatest worry so soon after his separation from Herta.

'Hi,' he said when he got home. 'Hi, Fips.'

He would call me Philipp, Fips or Filibuster.

He would take off his shirt, go over to the sink and wash his arms. He would then lather them with soap, dry himself and lay the table before clearing the plates into the sink as soon as dinner was done. He would then wipe down the waxed tablecloth and spread out the papers, letters and documents he took from a drawer in the living room cupboard.

When I saw he was completely absorbed, I would fetch my coat from the peg by the door and say, 'I'm off out again.' Casually, as if I didn't wish to disturb him but actually to keep to a minimum the hurt I caused him by going to see her. That was what it was: a recurring sense of hurt whenever I said, 'I'm off.'

He raised his head but didn't answer, didn't even nod but looked somewhere else, maybe sang one of those mindless tunes or picked up the rubber and rubbed out a word he had just written in the green book, and focused once more on his work, or at least pretended to.

The house where she now lived was, like all the houses in the street, clad with slate and roofed with slate, and it was towards a slate hillside that she looked out of the window when she got home at night. When she moved in in late summer, the stone was light grey, as if dusted with chalk, and in the autumn rain, water oozed out of it for a while after it had stopped raining; it seeped out from between the cracks, trickled downhill and ran across the yard in a small stream, a wet anthracite trickle that petered out between the sheds at the back of the yard. True, the January she disappeared, the slate had frozen. It was so cold that winter that the hillside was transformed into a sparkling wall of glass that reflected the lights from the window at night.

I remember that hillside and her landlady's dressing gown—a black dressing gown with silver stars and gold moons on it. This peculiar woman would sometimes open the door when I visited Herta, poking her head out of the door to stare at me. 'Oh, it's you,' she would say in a mumble caused by a poorly stitched-up tear in her upper lip.

As I said, she would sometimes open the door, but usually it was Herta herself. She would come to the door in her stockings and draw me inside.

'Come in,' she said, and I would follow her into the room with the sewing machine by the window and the table in the middle with the food she had bought during her lunchbreak spread out on it—fruit, crispbreads, milk, all on a ripped paper bag so the tablecloth didn't get dirty.

'Are you hungry?' she asked, to which I nodded as if to avoid reminding her that I had already had dinner at his, then picked up an apple and bit into it. When I pushed up my sleeves, I saw her staring at the scar on my left lower arm, the red line with the three red dots on either side of it, and thought she would mention that evening I'd followed her, but she didn't.

This continued through that summer, that autumn and half the winter. In the evenings when I was sure she had got home from work, I would run to her flat and stay there for an hour, and when I left, she would accompany me to the door or walk with me for a while, strolling alongside me as she had on the late-August afternoon I'm thinking of now. Her hair was bobbing up and down, the scent of her perfume was wafting over to me and after a while she slipped her hand under my arm so that we looked like a couple taking a stroll together—the lady and her young lover. On the bridge she stopped, leant over the balustrade and spat into the water. I stood by her side and looked at her sun-reddened face, her neck and her shoulders, which stood out under the fabric of her dress.

At the time it was as if the town were divided into two halves, one her turf and the other his, and the stream, the Taute, were a border not to be crossed. Or only in exceptional circumstances, in the mornings, when they went to work, and because she worked on his side and he on hers, a kind of territorial swap that was reversed in the evenings. He moved to her side and she to his. However, since they used different bridges—he the Amtsbrücke, and she the footbridge—and did so at different times, there was no danger of their meeting. They hadn't made any agreement and yet the Taute had become a border river that only I was allowed to cross, as a peace envoy or conveyor of news, sent out without any news and bringing none back. Or was I myself the news? She said goodbye to me on the bridge and turned back.

But on that particular day, in January now, a day of ice on and under the bridge, thick coats and gloves, having already let go, she linked arms with me again and carried on walking; she was entering enemy territory, showing no sign of turning back but striding firmly on, so I began to think she'd decided to come back, but then she stopped at the end of the road where the house with the fountain stood and glanced around, anxious all of a sudden, as if all at once she might spy him. It was an unfounded fear, though, because he wouldn't go out when he knew I was at hers and would wait for me to get home.

'And now, my friend,' she said, 'you will have to go on alone,' and after patting me on the arm, she turned back.

I set off again the next evening, down the stairs, along the street, over the bridge, up the other stairs, and pressed the doorbell twice. And I thought nothing of it when it was not Herta who came to the door but her landlady, the woman in the black dressing gown. The door opened a crack and her head popped out, her broad face with the tear in the top lip which revealed her incisors when she spoke, and she said with those incisors that she couldn't let me in.

'Why not?' I asked.

'Vy not,' she repeated. 'Vy not! Because she's gone.'

'Gone?'

'Moved away.'

'Where to?'

A shrug of the shoulders. And that was it, the beginning of something else. That shrug was the beginning of the time after. I didn't grasp this straight away, but it became clear to me on my way home. The woman shut the door and I went down the stairs, and just as everything on the way there had been part of beforehand, this was now part of afterwards. The lamps rocking on the steel cables over the junctions, the left-over Christmas tree with the candles swaying in the wind on the Obertor bridge, the crackle of the ice, the frozen cobblestones: it was all part of the after-time.

When I entered the kitchen, he was still sitting at the table, his face illuminated by the light reflected from the papers spread out before him, and he looked up in surprise.

'What?' he said. 'Back already?'

He put down his pen, a blue pen engraved with the name of Greiner's company. Strangely, keeping it didn't bother him. He wanted nothing more to do with the man, but he carried on using the biro with the man's name on it.

The sloping section between the steps and the fountain had frozen into a slippery slide, and now that the water had been drained from the fountain, a tongue of ice hung from the lion's mouth. On the way to school the next morning, I remembered a story that Axel had told while we were standing around the fountain. After one cold night, a beggar had been found dead on a park bench in Frankfurt, frozen into a block of ice so that it was impossible to lay him in a coffin and he had to be taken away in his sitting position with the utmost care because if he had fallen, for example while being loaded onto the lorry, he would have shattered into a thousand pieces like glass. And suddenly I knew what had happened. She had gone out again in the evening, as she some-times would. When she could no longer stand it in her room, she would go out to get some fresh air. She'd told me that she would wander the streets. And something had happened to her.

It was quarter to eight and still dark or almost dark. School started at eight. Before the courthouse I turned into the manor gardens, a slight detour, but I was drawn to the park, and spotting something on a bench, something black sitting there, my heart began to pound. She was sitting there. But as I came closer, I saw that it was something else, a black bag full of rubbish. I shoved it with my hand. It toppled over, and a bottle fell out and rolled across the path.

She's dead, I thought anyway; beaten or frozen to death. Until a few days later, that is, when Georg showed me the letter that had arrived that morning.

'Here,' he said, handing it to me.

I recognized her handwriting immediately. The letter was addressed to me, it was my name on the envelope, but he had opened it. Even though she knew I read the hardest books, she had cultivated a childish tone in her writing.

Dear Philipp, she wrote, *I am well. I have accepted a job that I like doing. The room I'm living in is nice and bright.*

The room I'm living in, she had written, but not the name of the town nor the address, which she kept secret. She didn't mention it in the letter, nor had she put it on the envelope. It was no different in this respect from the letters I received later on, from her cards and postcards. Later on, if you excluded the letter with the picture from the photo booth, I only ever received postcards, and they rarely said anything other than: *Dear Philipp, I'm well. How are you?*

That evening he went out again. He never went out in the evenings. He hadn't yet become invisible, but he never went out. When he got back from work, he would stay at home and sit, with his head propped on his hand, over his papers beneath the kitchen lamp, smoking and occasionally standing up and sitting down again. It looked very much as if it would be the same that evening. After dinner he wiped the table, fetched his papers from the dresser in the living room and spread them out. After sitting down, however, he got up again, took his coat from the peg by the door and said, 'I'll be back in a few minutes.'

I went over to the window and saw him step out of the shadow of the house. He moved gingerly, but all of sudden, just before the fountain, his arms shot up and flailed in the air as his legs slid out from under him, but he managed to catch himself, smoothed his coat, glanced up at the window and went on his way. Half an hour later he was back and put something on the table, an oblong box wrapped in brown paper and tied up with string, and attached to the knot was a label with my name on it.

He had gone back to the flat, to the woman with the harelip. She hadn't wanted to let him in. 'You have no business here!' she said with her incisors. 'Go away or I'll call the police!'

Yet he had shoved her aside and gone to the room at the end of the hallway, where he pushed the door open and looked around while the landlady stood in the hallway, yelling threats at him. The table with the lace cloth was once more in the middle of the room, the wardrobe in which her clothes had hung was empty, but on top of the wardrobe, too high for the landlady to spot, was a parcel with the label with my name on it. *For Philipp.*

'Open it,' he said.

I didn't want to, though. I had no intention of opening it. If she wanted to give me something, she should do it in person. As on the morning of his arrest, I was sitting on the corner bench with my elbows on the table and pulled a disdainful face.

'Oh go on,' he said, and when I shook my head, he sighed, went over to the kitchen cupboard, took out a knife, cut the string and tore off the paper.

What was inside? I can't remember. A book perhaps, a box of chocolates or a pair of gloves she'd spotted in her clothes store and liked the look of. Being well dressed was important to her, and so she wanted me to be well dressed too. Let's say then that it was a particularly nice pair of gloves that appeared and that I wore them for a few days and then forgot them somewhere, at school or in the stationery shop I regularly went to in the afternoons for a while. Its shelves boasted everything you needed for painting: pads of various sizes, tracing paper, coloured pencils and boxes of watercolours, charcoal sticks and the fixative you sprayed on drawings through a curved tube; they even had an easel in one corner. I went there and looked at everything because I'd started drawing. I removed my gloves when I went in and laid them on a shelf next to the pads.

*

'Gloves?' Mila said when I told her about this many years later while we were travelling, in Biescas where we had made a stop and I had set up my camera in the early evening at the nearby Ermita de San Juan de Busa to wait for the next morning.

'Gloves?' she said again, shaking her head. 'I don't believe you. It can't have been gloves. Think hard, Philipp. Think hard.'

It was clear that she wanted the parcel to have contained something else, a diary or a long letter (preferably in the form of a nineteenth-century novel of the kind in her father's library), a missive in which Herta explained why she had left or at least promised to explain one day, later, when I was old enough to comprehend her reasoning. But it wasn't. Not a diary nor a letter. I would have remembered that.

Just as other people wear baggy sweaters to hide their obesity, Mila wore baggy dresses to conceal her skinniness. She was wearing one when we first met at the theatre in the seventies in any case, and she still was that evening in Biescas when conversation turned to the two of them. She peered out from under her straw hat and kept shaking her head as she sipped her red wine, while the Gállego thundered past underneath the terrace where we were sitting; the water hurled itself against the stones jutting out of the riverbed, almost as spring meltwater used to turn the Taute in the slate town into a proper river for a few days.

From one of the notebooks I used on this trip:

M. —fragile, dainty, translucent, long-legged, long-necked, thin, thin-armed; her hands pick up objects between thumb and forefinger only, as if each was a delicate teacup . . . That's nonsense of course, but it creates an impression of primness which she is aware of and tries to counter with deliberately rough behaviour. Quietly. Her voice (for physical reasons?) never rises above the lower midrange, forcing me to ask her to repeat herself, especially in the car as we drive along the mountain roads—well, she usually drives. Making an effort to speak louder in response to my incipient deafness. A sense of gentleness. Deals between us? No, tacit agreement whereby each of us must do our best to support the other's game and on no account thwart it.

Why did I write this entry?

She used to sit through the meetings I sometimes attended at the theatre, hunched over and noting down every word. It was her first job, and she believed that every play included in the repertoire would prove to be part of a greater plan, which she called an over-all dramatic concept. Rubbish, I said. But she clung to this so earnestly that I came to the conclusion that she meant not only the repertoire (which, as she herself could observe, was in a permanent state of flux) but something else too, maybe a plan for life, and she got angry when I told her it wasn't so.

Her dramatic adviser colleagues walked around with little books poking out of their jacket pockets—the Groddeck. They used to say: in the Groddeck, Groddeck writes, it says in the Groddeck . . . If you walked into the cafe they went after rehearsals, you would see them sitting at a table, reading it, pencil in hand to make notes in the margins.

If they noticed you, they would raise their heads and look across, as if to check if what they had read could be applied to what they saw. Everything meant something—if you put your hand in your pocket, crossed your legs or touched your earlobe; and if they caught you in the act, they would smile as if they knew something about you that you didn't. Things were not what they were but something else, and Mila had been infected with her colleagues' interpretational zeal.

She had ditched this habit but continued to believe that nothing happened by chance.

'No Philipp,' she said, 'it isn't an accident,' when I told her about the blue letter. 'It's no accident that you woke up that night and followed Herta.' And the fact that her parcel contained nothing more than a pair of gloves? That was unimaginable for someone endowed with a sense of drama.

We had a short and passionate affair in the early eighties, only to conclude that we weren't right for each other. During this period, I had (how could I not have been?) an obsessional desire to photograph her, but the resulting pictures were as unsatisfactory as our romantic endeavours, which always ended in disappointment.

'It's my fault,' she would say as she turned away under me.

A minute earlier, she had clasped me with her arms and legs and thrust herself at me, seemingly smouldering with passion, but the next moment she would freeze and push me away.

For the first year after we met, she lived in Hamburg. We wrote long letters in which we declared our love for each other, our yearning and our desire, but during visits, we wouldn't pounce on each other but sit around demurely like two pensioners at tea-time, talking about plays, films and exhibitions we had seen or wanted to see.

Since I was on the one hand captivated by her looks and on the other knew that there was no point in rushing her—apparently, she needed time to move on from a previous lover, alluding to complicated relationship with an older man—I played along in the hope that I'd eventually be able to win her over. She was a few years younger and had, I heard on the grapevine, been involved with several famous men, all older. There was mention of an actor, a director and a publisher who, when I got to know them later, had all entertained the same hopes and felt just as fobbed off and disappointed as I had. The difference between us was that we (Mila and I) remained friends; indeed our friendship only really began once our relationship was over.

One explanation for this was perhaps that she was attracted to women, something which cannot have been news to her but must have only become completely clear during our breakup, and although it caused some initial aggravation, it had the advantage of setting boundaries. Even when she spent the night at my place or I at hers, or when she lived with me for a while or—as was frequently the case—we went on holiday together, it was obvious we would never be an item.

It was the east-facing rooms that I photographed or, more accurately, the morning light slanting into them. We drove around the country roads in Huesca province, stopping off in villages near half-ruined tenth-, eleventh- and twelfth-century churches. It was not the magnificent cathedrals of León and Burgos that interested me, but the tiny chapels dotted about the landscape like piles of stones.

We would arrive in the afternoon and while Mila searched for accommodation, I would go into the church, mark the spot where I intended to set up my camera and the next morning, while Mila was still asleep, I would set off, screw the camera onto the tripod and aim it at the window at the back of the apse. Sometimes it was placed high and narrow in the wall so that the light entered like the sudden flash of a laser beam; at others, it was shaped like a keyhole and the outline the light projected onto the opposite wall looked like a sword handle or a mushroom with a long stem. For a second the light outside the window seemed to explode, and the next instant it cast such a sharp image on the ceiling, the wall or the floor that I felt as if I might cut it out with scissors and take it home with me.

Apse or apsis, and apsides: I now know that the latter refers to the points of least and greatest distance of a planet from the star it orbits.

From the same notebook:

Rather than both disappearing into our rooms, as we tend to do, we stay sitting together for a while after the landlady closes the terrace, Mila on the bed with her legs pulled up, and it's then, as she pushes the lamp to one side and a ray of light falls for a second on her legs, that I see on the insides of her thighs, a hand's breadth below her crotch, a rectangular blood-stained plaster over two light-coloured, and therefore old, scars. Noticing my gaze, she pulls down her shirt.

And a week later, back in Germany:

Was the beige compact sewing machine back then, the thing that made a clatter in my memory, the same one she took on her travels? And the same one she brought back, now covered with transfers that made it possible to retrace her route?

14

We went on believing her absence was only temporary. Or I did, whereas my father had perhaps given up believing it but did nothing to disabuse me of my mistake. Quite the reverse: he maintained the optimistic expression that fed hopes of things turning out fine.

'Go for a spin': one of his expressions. Another one that she used too: 'Catch some air'. As if air was something you trapped in a net. A third: 'Time to kill.'

About a month had passed since Herta's disappearance when he came sprinting up the stairs. I was sitting at the kitchen table and heard him bounding up, the click of the front door and his voice calling from the corridor, 'Get dressed, Fips. We're going for a spin.' By this time, he was pushing the kitchen door open.

'A spin?' I asked faintly, putting my arm over the newspaper spread out in front of me.

'Yes. Quick!' he called, swinging his keys between his thumb and forefinger to urge me on.

Under the newspaper was a sheet of carbon paper and under that was a sheet of white paper, and in my hand was the pencil with which I had traced the silhouette of a beach babe lounging by the Mediterranean. Yes, I was tracing the outline of a woman— head, neck, shoulders, hips, legs—from the newspaper onto the

sheet below before removing the carbon paper and filling in everything her bathing costume obscured: nipples, belly button and the
mass of pubic hair. He craned his neck as he looked over at me,
but if he did spot the photo, he ignored it. He turned around and
went out into the corridor, giving me the chance to pack the newspaper, carbon paper and drawing away into my satchel, then he
came back with my coat and handed it to me.

'Get in,' he said as we stepped out of the house.

It was Schwepp's car—the Ford Taunus with the globe curving
out from the grill—parked by the fountain. He started the engine
and released the handbrake, all with the twinkling look of a dutiful
man temporarily shedding his inhibitions. We drove away down
the hill, out of town, taking not the main road but side roads, and
then uphill again past the slate quarries, deserted and dead in late
February (wounds that had been done to the hillside and had now
scabbed over), with glimpses of the small valleys that opened up
to the left and right of the road. I loved these drives, as he seemed
to cast off his unhappiness; concentrating on the road, on driving,
soothed him and softened his features.

Sitting beside him, I was happy to be near him, feeling a sense
of security I experienced neither at home nor anywhere else (let
alone at school) but only on these drives, alone with him,
enveloped by the faint smell of petrol, oil and rubber, and his own
scent of cigarette smoke and aftershave, accompanied by the purr
of the engine and protected by the steel skin that surrounded us
as we sat there, usually in silence, lost in thought.

I still don't know what had prompted this excursion. Was he
keeping a promise he'd made? Had he agreed to set aside the afternoon for me? I can't remember. I do know, however, that
something new began that day, a new phase of unhappiness.

We drove uphill for quite a long time before he eventually turned off at a restaurant about halfway up a peak. He pulled up, and we got out.

'Well?' he said, throwing his arms back at shoulder level to pump air into his lungs. 'Isn't it a beautiful day?'

It was a radiant, blue-skied day, the air so clear that we could see the white mountaintops all around, white not with snow but with frost on trees that sparkled in every shade of white; a day with a summery sky, except it wasn't summer, it was winter and icy cold, the wind cutting through my coat. We trudged up a narrow path. With every step you could feel the stone-hard earth under your shoes, the grass brushing against them with a crackling sound, and if you said something, the breath drifted from your mouth like smoke. It was about a 20-minute walk and from the top there were views in every direction; it was still light, but the radiancy had faded, the sun was trapped in a reddish haze and the sky in the east was slate-grey. He looked around and nodded.

'Are you hungry?'

'Yeah.'

'Come on then.'

We went back to the restaurant. We were met in the echoing vestibule by the aroma of food. He opened the door, cast an eye over the bar restaurant, turned on his heel and walked out. I don't know if he caught sight of someone he was determined to avoid or if he was put off by the number of people at the tables. It was dark now, and whereas our car had been the only one in the car park beforehand, it had since been joined by others. I automatically looked around for Greiner's car, the cream-coloured Bentley, but it wasn't there. Just a Mercedes, an Opel Kapitän and a few smaller cars.

He stopped when he reached the Ford Taunus.

'So, Fips,' he said, glancing at me uncertainly and taking the yellow packet out of his jacket pocket. He placed a cigarette between his lips, lit it and the next time he took it from his mouth, it stuck to his upper lip and tore off a tiny bit of skin, releasing a drop of blood which he dabbed away with the back of his hand and considered pensively.

'Oh well,' he said. And with that it began, which is why I mention this excursion. That was the beginning of his wounded time, which was followed by his invisible phase.

I say 'time' for lack of a better word, but I don't mean the time that passes, not time measured in days and weeks, but an accumulation of misfortunes that stands apart as a chapter in my life, punctuated only by the occasional short break; in the evenings, for example, when Schwepp would sometimes swing by from Siegen and brighten the gloomy mood with his clown face, smirking eyes and the upturned corners of his mouth. He would sit on the kitchen bench and play with his car key while Georg leafed through the files he had fetched from the living room.

Or, on some evenings we spent with just the two of us, he would sit at the kitchen table with a sheet of paper placed diagonally in front of him and write letters, with his fountain pen, of course—the green-and-black-striped one that had already been part of him in the canal town, the inkpot, the blue-stained sheet of blotting paper, the brown-leather pencil case with its press-stud clasp, two or three envelopes and the large grass-green book in which he made his entries after he'd completed his letter-writing, while one cigarette after another smouldered to an end in the saucer he used as an ashtray.

Had he smoked before? Before the chain of events set in motion by the sale (or rather: non-sale) of the camera?

'Yes,' said Lilo.

Herta's friend, whom I asked on my first trip to Plothow, confirmed this. Yes, he smoked, but only socially. He would light them with a certain show, wave the match out and toss it into the ashtray before inspecting the lit end, raising it to his lips, sucking in the smoke and letting it seep out of his half-open mouth with his head thrown back.

Long before the cigarette had burnt down, he would stub it out in the ashtray, although he now appeared to want to smoke the filter as well. His fingers, and in particular the tips of his thumb, index and middle finger, were stained with nicotine. His hands, his hair, his skin and his breath smelt of cigarette smoke; it had infiltrated his suits, his shirts and his sweaters, and also the curtains, the furniture and every other material or surface capable of absorbing the odour particles.

Where cigarettes had once been a means of enhancing the pleasure of a social gathering, after Herta's disappearance he appeared to need them to breathe, as if the air needed to be filtered through tobacco to enter his body and his lungs, as if the air he breathed in were only palatable if enriched with toxins. He always had a cigarette clamped between his fingers or his lips, or a cigarette smouldering on the ashtray or a saucer.

The days were lengthening, and increasingly the window was not open for a mere matter of minutes to evacuate the smoke but all the time, so we could smell the air, the earth and the wet slate.

At suppertime, he would gather up the papers he had spread out on the table, slide them into clear plastic folders and put them away in his brown briefcase—this was the sign for me to lay the table. I got everything out of the cupboard—wooden boards, cups and knives—and put it on the table while he filled the kettle to make tea.

Herta had moved away, but the habits she had shaped and the rules she had devised, remained. We continued to shop in her favourite stores, ate at the same times as we used to and sat in the same places, except for the fact that her chair had been pushed over to the window and was only moved back when we needed to put something down or if Schwepp paid us a visit.

There had been no change in my bedtime either, despite my best endeavours to have it pushed back. It became clear that he was just as much of a stickler for order as she had been. It may even have been that it was her departure that restored the order that had started to slide when she moved out. I had to be in bed at the latest by half past eight, and half an hour later he would come into my room to tell me to turn off the light; and at half past six in the morning I would feel his hand on my shoulder and hear his voice saying, 'Fips. Time to wake up, Fips.'

The kitchen table was already laid, the boards were in their rightful places, the bread was sliced, the jam jar unscrewed and milk was steaming in the pot; my clothes were hanging over the chair and underneath them were my freshly polished shoes.

It was as if by sticking to the daily routines so strictly he was respecting a legacy or a promise he had made to her, and I sometimes thought that their separation had come about by mutual agreement rather than as a result of a dispute, and he was only pretending not to know where she was but was actually in contact with her and receiving her instructions.

A few days after our excursion he picked up the bread, one of the large, crusty rye loaves from the bakery at the top end of the main street. He clasped it to his chest and held the knife to it to cut us a few slices, but the knife slipped and stabbed him in the heel of his hand. He jumped up, pressed a paper tissue to the wound and shook his head in disbelief.

On another occasion, he dropped a glass, which shattered on the floor, and when he bent down to pick up the pieces, as soon as he stretched out his hand when a splinter so tiny that he couldn't get it out bored its way under his fingernail. He cut the nail to just above his fingertip and poked around with a pair of tweezers but was unable to grip the splinter, which ate into his finger and festered. For several days, he dipped his hand in a homemade solution of soap and hot water, waggling his fingers back and forth, first to facilitate the inflammation and festering, then to disinfect the wound. From time to time he would take the kettle off the gas hob and add a little water; that water was his friend, until it too betrayed him. One morning, while he was making hot water, he knocked over the filter he had just filled with boiling water and, in his reflex attempt to catch the filter, scalded his other hand—the left one this time.

No sooner had his hands healed—these misfortunes always occurred when the consequences of the previous ones had sub-sided—than he came bounding up the stairs one evening, his foot slipped and twisted, and within a few minutes his ankle was so swollen that his foot no longer fitted into his shoe, and when it did eventually fit inside again, he couldn't do up the laces and had to leave the shoe undone, removing the laces so that he wouldn't trip over them.

The breadknife, the glass, the water, the stairs . . . They had become enemies and threats. He cut himself on them, slipped, scalded himself and twisted joints. He injured himself on everything, even on paper. Paper was another weapon that started to turn on him. Thin cigarette papers, and the sharp-edged paper of an envelope I took from the battered tin box one lunchtime after school—a large A4 envelope with a typewritten address, the sender a well-known company I'd heard of before.

Still wearing his coat, he came up to me, opened the letter by running his thumbnail under the flap, and as he took out the letter and held it up to the lamp, I saw that the curve under his thumbnail was filling with blood.

'Damn,' he cried, waving his hand in the air, dropping the envelope and running out of the room. I picked up the letter and skimmed through it. The famous company had written that unfortunately the position he was qualified for had just been taken.

The letter was so heavy because they had enclosed the documents he had sent in with his application: a handwritten CV and his employers' references. I went to look for him and found him standing by the living room window, whistling under his breath. He hadn't switched on any of the lamps and although it stayed light for longer in the evenings now, only the outlines of the furniture and his silhouette against the now faintly illuminated window were visible.

Where was he working at the time? Did he even have a job?

He left the house in the mornings and came back in the evenings, sat down at the kitchen table and turned on the radio on the shelf next to it. He had given up writing letters. He didn't send any, and none arrived. Instead he would suddenly leap to his feet and run from room to room with a duster in his hand, wiping the armchairs, the glass lampshades or the mirror in the hallway, but he no longer looked at his reflection. In the past I had occasionally observed him as he stopped in front of the mirror and looked at himself. Before he left the house, he would stand in front of the mirror, run his hand over his hair, fiddle with his jacket and only then open the door. He didn't do that any more.

He barely went outside anyway, except maybe on a Sunday, but he didn't go for a stroll like he used to when Herta was still there but for my sake, just as he borrowed Schwepp's car for my sake.

'Come on,' he would say in the evening when he realized we'd spent the whole day inside. 'Let's go outside and catch some air.'

It wasn't yet completely dark when we stepped outside. The children standing around the fountain looked up briefly and then away. They didn't see him, and he didn't see them. At the end of the street he didn't turn into the main street, for example, where the shops were, but into the narrow lane running behind it. Occasionally someone he knew would come walking towards us anyway, and he would cross over to the other side of the street. He offered no greeting and the other person didn't greet him either—maybe, I now think, not because people didn't want to greet him but because they didn't notice him. He would stick close to the houses, his hands deep in his duffel-coat pockets, and it is quite possible they simply didn't see him.

They saw me but not him.

'What is your job, actually?' I asked to start up a conversation.

'Oh,' he said, waving his hand as if chasing away flies. His hand shot up out of the shadow of the house and immediately vanished again.

'Oh!'

And once as were walking home along Heubachstrasse we saw Greiner. He was waiting outside the building, still the same one with the fountain outside, pacing up and down with his hands behind his back, though his car, the grey Bentley, was nowhere in sight, which meant he had come on foot. My father was wearing his duffel coat, the one made of shimmering red–green–blue material with leather buttons, and Greiner—as always when he wasn't dressed up as Lord Clifden—was wearing a three-piece suit made from what he considered to be the world's best fabric.

'Herr Karst,' he said as we approached.

This time too my father said, 'Go!' and shoved me in the back.

I went up the stone steps but not into the building, just to the front door where I stopped so I could overhear what happened next. It was his invisible phase, the time in which my father was invisible, and the fact that someone had come and said 'Herr Karst' was a relief to me, even if it was Greiner, his enemy.

The two men were about the same age and they also looked alike, both of them tall, their dark hair combed back. They only differed in their dress: Greiner in his suit, my father in a sweater and his duffel coat. He was standing there, and as Greiner took a step towards him and said something, he began to button up his multi-coloured coat. I couldn't hear if he was answering or busy with his buttons the whole time, but suddenly he turned and came up the steps behind me, while Greiner was left standing near the fountain, his arms hanging by his sides. Then he too turned and walked away along the street towards the stream, the factory, the house and the gazebo to which I had followed Herta.

Had he come to apologize? That's what I thought at the time: he meant to ask Georg for forgiveness. That's how I interpreted his attempt to talk to him. Yet when I think back to it now, I'm not so sure there wasn't another reason.

No, I don't have good memories of those days. Worst of all was Sunday, and the worst part of Sunday was the afternoon.

That Sunday, however, Georg said, 'Get dressed, Fips.'

I struggled up from the armchair in the living room where I'd been lazing around—I would usually sit sideways in it, with my legs dangling over one of the armrests, looking at a book—levered myself up onto my feet and shuffled into my room. I took off the tracksuit bottoms I wore around the house and put on the creased, grey flannel trousers, all this in slow motion while he was already waiting in the corridor in his duffel coat, which he wore all winter and spring.

Our destination was a restaurant by the Taute where we ate regularly now, every Sunday. Although I imagine we had very little money, it was part of our routine to go to the Lindenhof on Sunday afternoons, where we almost always ordered the same thing: schnitzel with peas and carrots and a slice of lemon in a flat stainless-steel press on the side of the plate. Through the window you could see across the stream to the school, the high school whose playground bordered the grey-channelled Taute, and our classroom window on the raised ground floor, the fourth from the left. I felt Georg's eyes on me as I peered over at it.

'Well,' he said, 'everything OK?'

'Yes,' I said, nodding.

The Lindenhof, Müller's restaurant, Ernst the butcher's: these were all the places where I had lunch because he had got a new job, one he could accept. He agreed on a price with the proprietors, and I went there after school, sat in the dining area and chose one of three set menus, until Frau Sacht, the grandmother of Bernd, one of the boys I sat around with on the iron railings outside our building, had a word with Georg. When she and her husband heard that I'd been having lunch at a restaurant since Herta's disappearance, they agreed this wasn't suitable for a child; they thought it would be better if I came to their house for lunch. Georg went along with this, and so I went to their place from then on.

They lived in a house at the top of the main street that would have fitted on a handkerchief but three stories high. Each floor had two small rooms, and the house had two entrances, the front one barely ever used. You went into the house through the back door and, passing through a tiny vestibule, came to the kitchen where the table would be laid when I got back from school.

Every day there was beef broth with little star-shaped pasta as the starter, then chicory or cucumber salad and, after a different main course every day, a bowl of stewed or preserved fruit from the garden. I stayed in my seat for a few minutes after eating. Frau Sacht would take off her apron and sit down with me. Her husband was a train driver and spent his whole career driving up and down the Dietzholz valley, always the same route. The railway tracks ran behind the plant where Georg had got his new job, and so Herr Sacht witnessed the changes in the valley at close quarters. It wasn't actually a plant yet, more like an enormous construction site with diggers and big-wheeled trucks cruising around on it, ripping up the ground, while teams of builders erected at great speed a hangar hundreds of metres long to house the rolling mill, the centrepiece of the entire works. Whenever Sacht, who despite his present technical vocation came from farming stock, described the plant, it was difficult to figure out if he felt joy or fear.

It was a long time since I had last eaten at their house, but I would sometimes knock on their door as I passed by, and Frau Sacht would open it, let me in and point to her husband sitting at the end of the table, staring straight ahead with a vacant, fixed expression. At her request I would give my news and she would stand behind her husband and run her fingers over his hair, always with precisely the same movement, until he eventually raised his eyes and looked at me.

'Oh, it's you,' he would say hoarsely.

Two years after his stroke they could no longer make it up the stairs to their bedroom—they were too steep—so they set up their bed in the living room from where they could look out of the window and watch people walking past in the street. It was a small window and low down in the wall, so you could usually only see people's torsos; the wall obscured everything else—their legs and their heads.

They both died the same summer that Herta returned. They were found lying in a close embrace on the sofa. When I ran into him once in town, Bernd, who had also joined the railways, told me that they had simply stopped breathing.

*

The green book—like an old friend. I happened upon it while having a peek into the moving boxes in the cellar. It was hidden between yellowing folders and files which mainly contained construction plans and bills related to our house, along with the correspondence with the board of the works; he had kept everything.

On the first page inside were his initials, G. K. Not a diary in the usual sense, more a place to keep notes, relatively disjointed and rarely dated; then messages to himself, notes to jog his memory, summaries of conversations, with Schwepp for example (regarding me, apparently: 'S. knows a boarding school in the Black Forest') or with Frau Wolf. And draft letters too, over and over again, the beginnings of missives to the defence ministry and, later, draft applications. Not a word about Herta though, only the address of her first flat, or rather of the furnished room in the harelipped woman's house. But then I found something, after all: not in the green book but in a black one he had obviously only started in recent years, which was lying next to the green one in the box: under the address of a gardener, from whom he had ordered, or intended to order, potting compost, was an account number, that of the home whose full name was noted above— *Martha Old People's and Care Home*, with an additional note, *For H. K.* There was something hasty and careless about his usually clear, tidy handwriting, as if he had had trouble keeping up with details someone might have dictated to him over the phone.

Did that mean that the man who refused even to pronounce her name had paid for her care? Despite living apart for over 40 years, they had never divorced. Or had he noted down the number because he wanted to make a donation to the institution? In that case, why this *For H. K.*, which looked like the payment reference?

An entry spread over several pages of the green book was, for once, marked with the date and told the story of Stoetzner. Georg read it in a magazine on offer at the hairdresser's the same autumn I was eating at the Sachts', and he recorded it in the green book in greater detail than he did other matters. Why? Because he knew the man in the photo? Because he was afraid the same might happen to him—kidnapped, abducted to the Soviet Union, sentenced to death and shot?

He believed that the man he had read about was the lawyer he had spoken to several times in Marienfelde camp after his escape, a neatly dressed little man with yellow nicotine-stained fingers. He was a member of the Liberal Lawyers, a group that had made it its business to siphon off information about East Germany and check the veracity of people's reasons for fleeing.

The man, whose name was abbreviated to St. in the article, was himself an East German and had been arrested and placed in custody in the early fifties in Erfurt, where he was staying with his fiancée, for careless, allegedly subversive speeches. He had, however, been able to escape through an open toilet window while being escorted to a doctor's appointment and had finally made it over the border to the West near Eisenach. Back in Berlin, but now in the western part of the city, he soon became one of the Liberal Lawyers' most prominent interviewers, driving his interviewees to despair with his perseverance and attention to detail, but what really made him a Stasi target were his articles accusing what was still known as the Soviet Occupation Zone of human rights violations.

Georg's only criticism of him was his smoking habits. He was a chainsmoker, lighting one cigarette after another, one still smouldering in the ashtray as he raised the next to his lips. He would sit there, veiled by a cloud of smoke from which his questions emanated, and Georg, who was of course a smoker himself, kept his own packet in his pocket in the man's presence and, as soon as he stepped outside again, would remove his jacket and wave it around to aerate it.

Stoetzner's smoking was ultimately his downfall. Fearing that he would run out of cigarettes during the night, he went downstairs again around ten at night to stock up from a vending machine near his flat. He was just pushing a coin into the slot when a man approached him from behind and asked for a light. As Stoetzner reached into his pocket for his matches, someone struck him on the head from behind. An Opel Kapitän fitted out as a taxi pulled up, the doors were flung open, and Stoetzner was dragged inside. He was still conscious and put up a fight, with his legs still hanging out of the door. The kidnappers bundled them into the car, but he kicked out at them and could possibly have broken free if one of his kidnappers hadn't pulled out a pistol and shot him in the leg; only then did they manage to slam the door and accelerate away.

His partner—not the woman from Erfurt who was suspected of having turned him in, but a former student friend and also a lawyer—had heard the noise as the car pulled up, rushed over to the window and witnessed most of what ensued: her lover's struggle with his kidnappers, the gunshot to his leg, the car racing away with a screech of tyres, how it almost collided with a delivery van at the end of Drakestrasse and, then, after swerving onto the pavement, sped off towards Goerzalle and Hindenburgdamm before (as was later worked out) crossing into East Germany near Teltow.

15

One evening, during what must have been the second year after Herta had left, a woman I didn't know came to visit him.

We were no longer living in the house with the fountain outside but in the one where the doors slammed. It was on the road leading out to the playing fields and was known as the 'skyscraper' because it was eight storeys tall and had a lift. When I lay in bed reading in the afternoons, I would sometimes hear a whistling sound from the corridors, immediately followed by a slamming and a banging as if doors were being flung shut all over the building, but when I looked outside I realized that it was the wind that was shaking and crashing the doors closed—a wind produced by the building, because another time, if you happened to look out of the window, you could see the poplars by the playing fields bent with the force of the real wind, although inside the building it was so quiet you could hear a pin drop.

He had just got home from work and his coat was still draped over the chair in the hallway (I could see it because I was sitting in the kitchen and the door was open) when the doorbell rang.

He opened the door and invited the woman inside. I saw her passing the kitchen on their way to the living room and since its door was also ajar, I watched her take a seat, remove a package from a bag and put it on the table. That is where it remained too, a package wrapped in grey paper; almost a parcel in fact, as tall as it was wide. He didn't ask what it was nor made any move to open it. They just sat there chatting, so quietly that I couldn't hear a word. He reached over once to put his hand on her arm, then immediately withdrew it again. After a few minutes she stood up, smoothed her coat and walked back along the corridor to the door, looking up briefly to nod to me as she passed. I didn't recognize her though. Even with the red scarf she was wearing, I couldn't figure out who she was.

He walked her out and when he didn't return, I followed them. Next to the lift was a narrow staircase leading downstairs, which was separated from the corridor by a grey iron door. I was about to open it when I spotted them through the small window in the door. They were standing on the landing, locked in an embrace. He had his arms around her and her coat had ridden up to her crotch while one of her feet was suspended in mid-air, like a quivering fish.

I sneaked back into the flat and into my bedroom, and when I came back into the living room a quarter of an hour later, the package was gone. There was a sound of clattering mugs coming from the kitchen; he was setting the table. He was as taciturn as usual over dinner.

'Who was that?' I asked after a while.

'Who do you mean?'

'That woman earlier.'

He looked at me in surprise. 'I thought you knew her.'

'But I don't.'

He thought for a second before saying, 'Someone I know.'

'And what was in that package?'

'Something that belongs to me.'

'Something?'

'A book.'

It wasn't though. It didn't look like a book. It was a square parcel, exactly as high as it was wide and deep.

Who did I think she was at the time? One of the women from his office, the barracks-like building that resembled an oversized construction hut and had gone up some time before the plant itself? When he took me there for the first time before Christmas, it still smelt of wood and fresh paint, and from the ceiling of the central corridor, which had six or seven rooms on either side, hung a neon tube casting a dim light.

He pushed open one door after another and, as the women pivoted on their chairs, said, 'May I introduce you to my son?' I noticed their eyes narrow and study me, as if they were trying to find a trace of his features in mine, and then a smile crept over the corners of their lips that made me insecure and made me want to leave. It smelt (another memory of my first visit there) of perfume and coffee, of gingerbread and peeled oranges. The draining board underneath the water heater was piled high with washed-up cups. I shook everyone's hands, and we moved on to his room at the far end of the corridor.

Through the window, illuminated by powerful spotlights, I could see the steel skeleton of the half-built rolling mill, whose name was already marked on signs by the roadside.

'Look,' he said, pointing outside.

Frail snowflakes drifted through the air. The soil ploughed up by the trucks laden with heavy concrete parts had frozen and was coated with a layer of white hoarfrost. There was a knock on the door, and the women I had said hello to came in one by one, clustering in the doorway. The last to appear was a chubby young

man with horn-rimmed glasses that had slipped down his nose—
Herr Loewis, his assistant. He was carrying an Advent wreath with
four lit candles.

Yes, it had been not long before Christmas when he took me
along to the plant for the little party they had organized, but it
wasn't one of the women I saw that day who came to see him at
the house with the slamming doors. Old and young alike, they all
seemed driven by the same desire to please him.

If you looked at his hands during a conversation, you would often
think he'd clenched them into fists, but looking more closely, you
would see that the thumb was not curled around the fingers as
usual in a fist but covered by them, as if to protect the thumb (his
fingers were also only slightly bent inwards), which upended your
impression. A minute earlier you thought you had before you a
man who would do whatever it took, who never shirked a con-
frontation, but now you saw an inward-looking man in search of
protection and therefore in need of protection—although this was
just as misleading.

At the time, I used to draw invisible portraits, tracing the facial
outlines of the people I saw with my finger. Forehead, nose,
mouth, chin. My hand would be resting on the table, apparently
still, and yet it sketched (as if compulsively) the shapes with tiny
movements only perceptible in my fingertips—a drawing motion
that was carried out on the smallest of areas but no less strenuous
than real drawing would have been. It was also during that period
that I began to see people's glances, the glances they gave one
another, the overt and covert looks that passed between them.

He used to pick me up from school at Saturday lunchtime. I
would get into his car and we would drive along the stream to
Bismarckplatz where he parked. We would go into the butcher's,

the baker's and the greengrocer's. It was shortly after one o'clock, a time when everyone was out and about, even women who were never seen in town on a weekday. They hurried along the streets with their shopping baskets hanging from their arms. And that's when I would notice them, the glances he exchanged with them. Informative glances, always accompanied by an amused arching of eyebrows or a barely visible nod, by which, I worked out, he made dates or learnt that it would be impossible to honour an agreed rendezvous. If I turned around, I might find myself looking into a face that was staring at him and, if only I looked around, that face would quickly avert its gaze.

The annoying thing was that I noticed these glances not with one woman but with several, and so the lines I had been accustomed to follow got crossed and after a while I had the feeling that the whole town was crisscrossed by glances like taut wires.

It was then too that, having not been given the camera I had asked for for Christmas, I began to write, first on the blank pages of old school exercise books and then in one of the small, linen-bound notebooks they sold at the stationery shop. I had taken to walking through the streets with my jacket or coat collar turned up and my hands stuffed into my pockets, as there was nothing to detain me at home. Now and again I would stop, take out my notebook and jot down anything I deemed worth recording.

I had got into the habit of imagining I'd committed the crimes I read about in the newspaper. When it became too much of a strain for Frau Sacht to cook for me, I went back to eating at the restaurant on Bismarckplatz where Georg booked lunch for me. The first thing I did after entering was to get my hands on the newspaper. I would take it down from the clothes peg from which it was hanging, lay it next to the napkin with the cutlery on top and open it at the page with the miscellaneous items of news featuring reports of the crimes committed in the area. I read them before my meal arrived, while I was eating and then afterwards, until they cleared my plate away. I studied every single article and behaved, as soon as I stepped back out into the street or roamed around during the afternoon, as the perpetrator would have done. I stuck close to the houses and kept glancing back, constantly expecting to feel a sudden hand on my shoulder arresting me, or to hear handcuffs clicking shut on my wrists. It wasn't me, I would say as they arrested me, but in a voice no one would ever believe. So far I was toying with my pursuers. If I noticed myself getting tied up in knots during questioning, which I envisioned as a series of complicated dialogues, just as I was unmasked I would switch back to being the innocent citizen I was, and watch what happened to my criminal alter ego in horror: how he was arrested and turned over to the judicial system, where he would be dragged under by a whirlpool of injunctions.

How old was I? 15? 16? If I knew that Georg was going to get home late from work, I would go out again and hang around in the bars near the station and the playing fields and behind the freight warehouses, in pubs frequented not by school pupils but workers and lorry drivers. I would sit down in a corner, order a rum and coke, take out the linen-bound notebook and listen to the hubbub of voices at the bar. I would catch the words that drifted over and store them like contraband in my book; and once I looked up and saw Kriwett sitting with a beer a few tables away, staring at me.

'I know you,' he said when he felt my gaze. 'Aren't you . . . Yeah, that's it.' He searched for my name but he couldn't remember it, and so he dismissed the matter with a wave of his hand, got up and staggered out and, following him, I spied him sitting on the kerb a little further up the road. He was trying to get to his feet, but he kept slumping back to the ground. I pulled him up, grabbed him under the arms and led him across the street to where it sloped down to Greiner's premises. The sign over the entrance still said *Textile Factory*; but not only was it not a textile factory any more, it wasn't a textile dealer's either. Greiner had scaled down the company more and more and made people redundant until only Kriwett was left in charge of the yard, the cars, the house and the garden; Greiner had sacked everyone else. People said he spent less time in his house by the Taute than in the one by the Thames—not in London, but somewhere called Twickenham, farther up the Thames—until these reports also turned out to be wrong.

I stopped at the entrance and watched Kriwett walk over to the house, his body at a slight angle, as if leaning into the (non-existent) wind, then he opened the gate and vanished between the bushes.

16

In the evening I picked up Mila from the station, as she was stopping off in Frankfurt on her way back from a tour somewhere. She had arrived by plane and was originally planning to travel straight on to Berlin by train, but then she rang to ask if she could stay for a few days. Of course she could. And could I meet her at the station? I could. When I got to the station, I saw the reason for her request.

She was walking towards me as I was on my way to the platform where the trains arrived from the airport. Glued to her side was a pudgy little girl in flowery culottes who was chatting incessantly to her and only stopped chattering when I caught hold of Mila's arm. She raised her eyes, which had been staring at the floor the whole time, and looked up at me from under her dreadlocks—yes, dusty dreadlocks, spotty forehead, purple blouse. She was wide-eyed and bewildered, and no, not as young as she had seemed—wrinkled forehead—and then her eyes moved on to Mila, who was smiling amiably to herself with that unshakeable, self-absorbed smile; and now the other woman exploded or rather something exploded inside her, for the only outward sign of this was a hiss.

'I don't believe this,' she cried, glancing back and forth between Mila and me. 'I really can't believe it.' Then she burrowed her way through the crowd and ran up the escalator.

'Annette?' I asked. '*The* Annette?'

But no, it wasn't; Annette was ancient history. It was a different assistant. Or an actress? That's right: an actress.

'Very talented,' Mila said and handed me her bag while she rolled her suitcase along.

Next morning, as long planned, I go to Tautenburg. Mila is exhausted after three weeks in Japan but she's too anxious to sleep, so she comes along. She rests her head against the car window and shuts her eyes, but every time I think, *Now she's asleep*, she opens her eyes again and blinks furiously.

'Just sleep!' I say.

However, she only went to sleep when we arrived in Tautenburg. As I was going round opening the blinds, she sat down on the sofa in the living room and by the time I peeked in a little later, she had slumped onto her side and was breathing deeply with her eyes closed.

His notes were everywhere. He had written notes with a biro in his neat, upright handwriting, usually only a few words long. *Call P.* or *Rain all day*. They were all over the place—on the console in the hall, on the kitchen cupboard and the TV, next to the phone. One of them said: *Buy wood preserver*. Another: *Ask doctor about blood sugar level*. He had kept a record in these notes of all the things he mustn't forget and ended each with an exclamation mark that looked as final as if he had tried to engrave it on the paper with a chisel.

Then, on his desk, was another piece of paper that didn't contain a reminder but what were clearly notes about a dream: *R., a pretty island all of a sudden. The cars have all disappeared. I walk along the water. In the distance, two people in sand yachts (a man and a woman?) are closing at great speed on a thin wire stretched across the beach that will, I know, cut them in half. I shout and gesticulate, but they pay no attention. At the last moment, I lift the wire so they can race underneath it. The way they look round once they're beyond it, the way they laugh. I look at the clock and say,* What a pity—by this time tomorrow I'll be dead. *No fear, only regrets because it's so wonderful right now.*

This note was weighed down on the front edge of the desk by the penknife he normally used for opening letters; or to be more precise: these two notes, for there were two of them stapled together. On one of them the dream, on the other just two words: *Her hour.* Whatever that meant.

Was he referring to a specific island? Rømø, where his Danish friends had a house that he sometimes went to?

All of a sudden—that must mean he didn't usually think it was beautiful. So why did he go there then? To see his friends, the people he'd been billeted with during the war? He painted it as a close friendship when he talked about them, but he never stayed for more than one night. He would drive to Tondern, where they lived, deliver the brandy they obviously expected as a gift, spend the night and then drive on the next morning to the house they kept free for him.

One time he was planning another trip there, he rang me up and said, 'You could come along.'

That was his manner of expressing his wishes. He didn't say, 'Come with me!' but formulated it cautiously, exploratively, in the conditional, as a possibility, as if he was scared of pestering you if he voiced his wishes too clearly. That was the last thing he wanted and that is precisely why he got his way.

August '75? Maybe that's right. The speech was from around that time, '75 or '76.

I had just arrived and was standing in the kitchen. He'd put some water on to boil for coffee when we heard a shrill bang and, looking round, we saw that the metal ring around the hob had snapped. It was lying in two halves on the top of the stove. A misfortune of this kind would usually drive him to despair (it was a sign that the whole world was against him), but that day he merely shrugged, turned off the hob and moved the kettle to a different one.

The house nestled between low hills covered with marram grass beyond which you could see the roofs of the other houses. The Danish flag was flying in front of some of them, a white cross on a red background, and beneath them people had parked their Saabs and Volvos, although you only saw them when you left the haven of your own home. A path led through the hills to the beach which he described to me as the widest he'd ever seen.

'Good. Let's go to the beach,' I said, but he didn't want to.

'It's too early.'

Why was it too early? But then, when we reached it, I saw why. The beach, which was indeed wider than any I knew, was one gigantic car park. The cars had been driven down almost to the waterline, people were sitting under awnings they had set up alongside their vehicles, an ice-cream vendor was wandering around, and whereas the beach was white sand up by the dunes, it darkened more and more into a grey, pounded track the closer you got to the water. Basically, you could only use the beach before the day-trippers arrived or after they had left again.

So that was where his dream was set. That was where his dreams took him back to many years after his last visit to the island.

No, it wasn't a pretty island, not even in retrospect, which is why I pretended to have a meeting and drove on the next day to Sylt.

There was a ferry every two hours from Havneby to List—a stone's throw. If you were standing on a slight rise—for example, on the quay wall—you could see the northern tip of the next island; the ferry took 40 minutes. People barged their way onto the ship, sat down at the restaurant tables and waited for the ship to cast off so they could order fish from the agitated waiters and then wolf it down before they got to List. It was a ferry, but it was also a food-and-booze cruise; the Germans ordered fish platters of herring, eel, salmon and shrimps, the Danes bottles of aquavit.

He warned me beforehand. 'Don't go to a restaurant. If you want to eat fish, buy it at the harbour.'

When he took me to the ferry, he pointed me to the shop opposite the jetty, waited until the ferry had left and then drove back to the house among the dunes.

I'd told him that I was going to stay on Sylt for a day, but then one became three, and on the evening of the second day I saw him at the end of the beach road leading to the promenade in Westerland—him and the woman who had visited him many years before in the house with the slamming doors.

They were walking towards me in the pedestrian zone, clearly on their way back from the beach, he with a camping bag over his shoulder and she with a rolled-up towel in a string bag, which she tossed first over one shoulder and then the other.

This time I recognized her immediately. She was walking a few metres ahead of him, but then he overtook her and as he passed, she brushed his arm with her hand, upon which he stopped and she walked past him. I had observed all of this once before, on a class outing to Marburg I had joined at his request, the same ballet, the same pussyfooting around each other; and just as then, as soon as I spotted them I ducked into a shop doorway and, hidden by a postcard stand, watched them walk past before stepping out again and gazing after them.

She stopped in front of a shop. He glanced over at her but eventually he turned and walked out of the pedestrian zone across a road, sat down on a bench and rested his arm on the back of it while she walked up to a car parked at the side of the road and got in. I wasn't so sure now. Was it really her? Lisa? A man was sitting in the car, waiting for her; not Greiner—they had divorced long ago—but a different man with a grey crewcut. She leaned over and gave him a kiss on the cheek.

But then, as the car pulled away, she wound down the window, dangled her hand outside and stretched out two fingers as a sign to Georg, to which he nodded and raised his hand slightly, and when the car turned into the square, I saw its registration—MR for Marburg. And then I realized what the phone conversation had been about.

We had just got back from our walk on the beach when the phone rang. He had picked up the receiver and I heard him say, 'What? You're here already?' He had sounded surprised. I was standing next to the phone table in the living room and turned away from him towards the window overlooking the dunes we had tramped up.

Now I understood how the two things were connected. She had called—Lisa. She was holidaying with her second husband on Sylt and was making the most of the opportunity to meet up with Georg. He clearly hadn't reckoned with her being there, not yet. He'd wanted me to visit him, and now she was there earlier than planned. Which is why he hadn't protested when I told him the next morning that I'd be moving on. I don't mean to suggest he was happy about it, but it did make it easier for him to meet up with her.

The kinship of lovers—an entry in his notebook from around the same time. Inspired by him? What this probably meant was that the relationship remained intact even when the love was gone. Lovers as a form of family, held together not by ancestry but by memory. His girlfriends—what were their names? The secret dates he arranged with them, the routes to the hotel, the guesthouses on the forest edge, the evenings, the nights, early mornings gazing out of the window while the other was still asleep, the car-park farewells, or the absurd dance he had performed in the pedestrian zone with Lisa (or Lisa with him)—were these not things that bound people together more tightly than kinship did through afternoons with the family, a shared grandfather, a senile uncle, a sister claiming the whole inheritance for herself?

Yes, I thought, until I visited him in Tautenburg, and we walked through town together. The same women came walking towards us; they looked up briefly, but the spark was gone and the wires had been clipped; his phone, which didn't stop ringing for a while, had fallen silent. And I knew then that it was over. Yes, that it hadn't even required a decision; it had just happened. It was clear that the couples had as little power to prevent waning erotic tension from breaking up their relationships as the lovebirds had exerted over their budding passion, their dreams of the future and their resulting sense of belonging.

17

The sea—for the first time with the two of them, him and her, starting from Plothow, the year before the slate town, when everything was still fine from the boy's point of view: a marginal sea that they had studied beforehand under his guidance, not a serious one; a puddle compared to the real sea, and yet still treacherous enough to attempt to murder him, the father who was still called nothing but Papa.

The journey: a protracted dream of flashing trees, meadows, coal dust, the hiss of steam, small-town stations (where the train often stopped long enough to buy confectionery at the station kiosk), jostling crowds and droopy-eyed tiredness . . . Soon after Berlin, the anticipation begins. Where is it, where's the Baltic? After every forest they pass through, behind every bend and dip, I think I can spy it, detecting an omen in every waterway, every pond, every little river shimmering in the distance. Is that it? Or at least a part of it? Yet after a great deal of futile peering, there's still a change to negotiate, from the big train onto a small one, and our journey continues under a cloud of black steam along a never-ending avenue, past wooded hills beyond which it really is supposed to lie—the sea. The sandwiches have long since been eaten, the water bottle is empty, there's a smell of apples and apple peel, of soot, cigarette smoke and dirty toilets; there's no water for handwashing, and the unravelled rolls of toilet paper lie trampled in disgusting puddles on the floor.

The father has also been looking out of the window for a while now. He pulls the boy towards him, so he ends up standing between his father's legs, and there it is: it is visible in a V between hills, the pale green-yellow surface of the sea, blurry in the haze of the afternoon sun. It is immediately obscured by a hill but appears now at ever-decreasing intervals. The door to the vestibule, previously only opened when someone wanted to move between carriages, stays open now; the air that comes in still smells of soot, but it has a new, fresh tinge to it, a tinge of promise. The train has slowed down and lets out a series of high-pitched whistles. They pass houses and a lowered barrier where people in swimming costumes wait, sandals on their feet, towels over their shoulders.

Then, at last, they are there. The boy, wide awake again, scrambles to get out, but his mother restrains him. Wait, she says. Only when the others have disembarked and the carriage is almost empty do they stand up, the mother casually smoothing her skirt, the father stretching his legs and fetching the suitcases down from the luggage rack. Come on, he says, let's go. They climb down from the train and exit through the semi-circular station into the afternoon sun; the forecourt is paved with large stones, the sun is shining on a circular flowerbed in whose centre are two banners marked *Thanks to the activists* and *Sunshine for every child* to greet those arriving; the first attempted photos, not by them but by people from their carriage who recognize them and wave.

Their last holiday together, and the first I really remember. They stay in a kind of villa with many rooms including a large dining room. Clusters of chandeliers hang from the ceilings, and six long glass doors with rounded tops lead out to a terrace dotted with parasols, tables and chairs, from where steps descend to large gardens criss-crossed with light-coloured gravel paths shining in the twilight; in front of a hawthorn hedge stands a head-high sculpted shell from which the paint is peeling.

All the rooms in the house are occupied. Nevertheless, this isn't a hotel but a trade-union holiday centre where, with Kabusch's intercession, the father managed to book a room for himself, his wife and their boy a year ago. In the evenings the corridors echo with the voices of people going out to the concert at the casino or to an event in the building advertised on a poster, a cabaret evening in the dining room, which was rearranged in the afternoon for that purpose; the faces under the freshly washed hair (the men's hair is often still wet and neatly parted) are red from the afternoon sun, and sun cream has been applied to bare arms and legs after showering, so a sweet-scented cloud hangs over the audience's heads once the doors have been closed.

When not at the beach, Georg generally wore trousers, held up by a woven leather belt and flapping with every step, and a white open-necked shirt with the sleeves rolled up to the elbows. He tanned easily and so there was a light stripe of skin on his left wrist where his watch usually was. I see her, Herta, in a flowery blouse and flared skirt with sandals on her feet, sitting on a low wall and squinting down at the camera. Her dishevelled hair in the wind. They took photos of each other and many snaps of the boy: in the water, astride a seesaw, apparently asleep in the canopied beach chair, holding on to his mother's arm as she presses her brow to his hair, or with him, Georg, beside a boat that has been dragged up onto the beach, both of them taming their wind-blown hair with their left hands.

These pictures, five centimetres by five with serrated edges, are stuck in a red leatherette-bound album I was given years ago, the top left-hand corner of its pressed-straw cover imprinted with a

boat thronged by gulls and, in the bottom right, the inscription
Heringsdorf Seaside Resort.

Meals, I recall, were not served by waiters but handed out through
a hatch at one end of the dining room where a long line formed;
instead of leaving your empty plates on the tables, you carried
them over to a trolley against the wall by the hatch. Sometimes it
was Georg who queued, sometimes Herta, while it was my job to
defend our table, and when Georg queued on his own and came
back with the tray on his own, a woman would sometimes look
round at him, causing Herta—if she twigged—to shoot me an
amused glance.

One of the women at a nearby table looked over at regular
intervals. Her laughter made me laugh too, and one day I noticed
Georg greeting her, which is to say he nodded to her, and another
day I caught him talking to her. I was coming back from the toilet
when I spotted him at her table, holding her hand, while Herta
stood at one of the six doors to the terrace, looking over at them,
her bag on the tiles at her feet. She was just bending down when
a fat man appeared beside her, took her arm and led her through
the doorway, and as they crossed the dining room, I recognized
Kabusch. He was in Greifswald, he said after we had sat down at
the laughing woman's table, to take part in a meeting lasting several
days. He had taken this afternoon off to visit his wife, the laughing
woman, who had known whom she was sitting alongside the
whole time without disclosing her identity.

His wife? Yes, I think that is how Kabusch introduced her. Or
his colleague? Secretary? Lover? She was the reason he had come,
but there was a second one: Georg. He had also come to see him
for advice about some business being negotiated in Greifswald.

And so Herta and I went to the beach on our own, without Georg, who stayed behind with Kabusch and the laughing woman.

We went back up to our room. Herta rolled up the towels that had been hung over the chairs to dry and put them into her raffia bag. I shut the windows, and we went downstairs again. The wind blew through the long, sickle-shaped grasses along the path. After a time, the wickerwork beach chairs, surrounded by a wall of sand, appeared between two dunes. Near the shore the water was yellowy green, further out it was stone grey and on the occasional stormy days, dark black. On those days, the Baltic Sea would roll in with foaming white crests, and the wind batted flakes of this foam back and forth across the wet, pounded sand when the waves retreated, along with polished pebbles, seaweed, jellyfish and the odd piece of amber the size of a fingernail; and the black ball, which usually hung a third of the way up a tall pole next to the lifeguards' wooden tower, was raised to indicate that no one should go into the water. This was rarely the case, however, as the weather was fine. We waded into the water together, and Georg taught me to swim.

'No need to be afraid,' he told me the next day when Kabusch and the laughing woman had left again. He lay on his back, spread out his arms, waggling his hands slightly (he kept his legs together, with the tips of his toes poking out of the water) and let himself drift around on the small waves. 'See, you float.'

Then he turned onto his front and sketched a few strokes by reaching forward with his arms and performing a shovelling movement past his head and back towards his body until they were by his thighs before pulling his arms up to his chest and propelling them forwards again while his legs opened and closed in synchrony, like a frog's. That's exactly what it looked like.

'Your turn now.'

They practised the whole morning until the boy had lost his fear and was ready to follow his father out into the deeper water where he could just about stand; and then, with his next thrust, he was suddenly out of his depth. They swam alongside each other for a while, and when he got water in his eyes and they began to sting so badly that he could no longer concentrate on swimming, they waded back to the shore where Herta was waiting for them with a towel. She rubbed the boy down, and the father dragged the beach chair around to face the sun again and the water where he had almost drowned that afternoon.

From the outside the house where they were staying looked enormous—a castle, a palace. Yet their room was tiny. A double bed for the parents, a folding bed for the boy, a table, a chair and a wardrobe: that was all there was space for, not forgetting a washbasin with a tap that produced a trickle of cold water. The showers were across the corridor, but the room did have a small balcony looking out onto the grounds, beyond which a strip of beach was visible.

For the afternoon nap, the balcony door, which was otherwise open, was closed, and a pleasant twilight fell over the room where, unexpectedly (naps having been abolished at home), they all settled down for a sleep after the morning's strenuous swimming and lunch downstairs in the dining room. He flicked through 'Bluebird', Anna Jürgen's story about American Indians, which he had brought with him, but before the words could hook him, he slid into a deep sleep from which his father woke him an hour later, and they set out again soon afterwards . . . To the pier or Gorky's house, depending on the weather but, on that particular day, it was to the beach.

The yellowy-green water by the shore. The waves lapping gently at the beach. The sun hiding in a hazy sky. Georg has just trudged across the sand, then a little way through the diminishing waves and into the water, alone because they, Herta and the boy, would rather stay warm in the shelter of the beach chair and the wall around it, but she sits up and watches Georg walk through the surf, lie on his back after the first shallow waves and let himself drift before twisting onto his front and swimming out to sea. She's used to this, she knows he's a good swimmer who loves to float around on the swell, and so she sinks back down onto her towel and when she looks up again, she sees him waving far out, sees his outstretched hand, and she waves back only to jump up and take a closer look. Is he really waving? Or is he beating the water? Yes, he's slapping the water with his arm, and what she's watching is no longer waving but a struggle. He's struggling against something that has caught hold of him; what she sees is a cry for help, and by the time she turns in panic towards the lifeguards' tower, two life-savers are already sliding down the pole, running across the beach and diving into the water. They do a fast crawl out to the struggling swimmer. It's a long way, so far that the two lifeguards sometimes vanish between two lines of breakers before reappearing and at last they reach him, at long last, and pull him out of the vortex that had formed beneath him.

Later, they were able to reconstruct what had happened. A sudden sucking that caught hold of him and threatened to drag him under, a maw that opened on the sea floor, a sudden gaping gorge, connected by conduits to the depths of the Earth, that wouldn't allow him to twist his body horizontal and, with powerful strokes and kicks, escape its snapping jaws. That's why he required those two young men to grab him from both sides and drag him to the beach, where he collapsed onto his back and lay there, gasping for air.

The beach was closed the next day. The black ball on the pole beside the lifeguards' tower had been raised in warning, and bathing along that stretch of beach was forbidden until further notice.

The sentence in the green book was: *Must go around as a rescued man for the rest of time.* Just that, unrelated to any of the writing before and after it.

One photo stands out not only because of its format, 10 by 15 centimetres, but above all due to its mood. Both of them dressed up, which is to say that he is wearing a suit and tie and she a sleeveless blouse and a string of pearls, their faces tanned and shiny, not from nut-oil sunscreen, but as if from an excited, wine-fuelled conversation, from planning, discussions about the future, the promise of happiness, so that not even the holiday rep in the polar-bear costume standing between them, arms draped around their shoulders, can disturb their harmony; they simply smile him away with their hopes for future bliss.

The boy is not in the photo. He's missing not only from the picture but also from their gestures, their eyes and their intimacy; his absence is palpable.

*

I came back from the Baltic Sea with a Finnish knife that had been on display in a souvenir shop window—a nice-looking, slender knife with a light wooden handle and a long leather sheath that Georg bought me, against Herta's will, when I wouldn't stop grizzling; whereas Mila brought back stones from her first trip to the Baltic—lumps of amber, quartz and pebbles she picked up from the beach under her father's supervision and has kept in her childhood bedroom to this day, in a small chest of drawers by the window.

When she invited me there for the first time, we climbed a sweeping wooden staircase and she opened a drawer, took out a flat black stone with a hole the size of a pinhead in the middle and gave it to me.

'An adderstone,' she said. 'It brings good luck.'

'Why?'

She didn't know. She couldn't tell me why it might do that or how it got its name.

When we came back downstairs, her father was standing there looking at us. A short man with a round face, he was a lawyer and a booklover who collected first editions—Fontane, Thomas Mann, Döblin, the great storytellers—and whose library was arranged not alphabetically but by year of first publication. He screwed up his eyes and studied me, as if he were wondering what to make of the man his daughter had brought home, an illiterate person who carried a camera case around with him. Behind him was the beaming face of his other daughter, Christine, who had come over from New York with her husband Bill. She was sitting on the sofa between her children, the twins, whereas Bill was standing in the doorway a little to one side, in his red jacket. He was staring at the tips of his shoes, but then he looked up and winked at me, as if to say, 'Don't worry about it!'

Just then the doorbell rang and the other guests came in, laden with small gift-wrapped parcels, which Mila's father accepted with a smile.

'I'm not going to open them now. Tomorrow,' he said, placing them on a low table his wife had placed next to the fireplace that afternoon and covered with a white cloth.

His birthday was actually the next day, but the party was that evening. More and more guests came in, and soon the high-ceilinged room with the Biedermeier furniture, the piano and the bookshelves, lit by lamps sunk in the ceiling, was filled with a regular hum of voices. People stood around chatting with glasses in their hands and, all of a sudden, I thought of my father and the silence that encased him like a corset, and I longed to leave, to go out into the street.

The camera was in the boot of the car. On the way there, we had driven past an old barracks, a long brick building with broken windows, which fitted the series I was working on. I collected derelict factories, hospitals, schools and railway stations, public buildings that had once teemed with people and life and now stood empty and crumbling. As I searched for a way to slip away unnoticed, Mila appeared and drew me into an adjacent room where the buffet had been set up. Her mother was standing at the end of a long table, pointing to the platters and dishes.

'That is rabbit pâté,' she said, 'and that's a cheese bake.'

I picked up a plate, but then put it back and went outside.

The barracks lay between blocks of flats on a long road connecting the town to Hamburg.

It was late June, still light, and the sun was shining on one end of the brick building, while the long side wall was in shadow. The open door had '1889' engraved above it. I stepped into a gloomy staircase, climbed up to the first floor and walked along the hall-way. The walls were sprayed with slogans such as *Buy fear!* and *Never forget Angela!* The floorboards in one room were charred, as if someone had attempted to light a fire there; someone had put a condom on a door handle, and in one corner were some beer bottles and two tattered blankets, both also singed.

I wandered around, took my pictures and went back downstairs and, stepping outside, I spotted a phone box on the other
side of the road. I hesitated for a second, but then I crossed over,
went in, opened the phonebook and looked under K. I hadn't done
this for years. It used to be the first thing I would do when I arrived
in an unfamiliar town. I'd look up whether the name Karst was in
the phonebook. Without thinking about it, I assumed that my
mother was still alive and still had the same name as when she disappeared. I did it one more time the day I met Mila's parents, then
never again.

It was still light when I got back. Bill was sitting on the porch steps.
He'd removed his jacket and laid it over his knee, and rolled up
his sleeves so you could see the ginger hairs sprouting from his
arms, the freckles and the glassy skin.

'When are you gonna come and see us?' he asked, as I sat down
next to him. But his eyes said: *I know you won't.*

Mila was standing with Christine and the twins by a small
pond hemmed with fieldstones. The two women bent down to
pick up the girls and dangled them over the water as if they were
going to drop them in. The children screeched. Looking up, I
noticed Mila. Her eyes said: *You left. I brought you along, and you
just upped and went. That's not on.*

Back then, at the end of the seventies, she was still playing the
role of the daughter who inspired the highest hopes, and that
meant not only having a successful career (the very least that was
expected) but also getting married and having children, which in
turn meant finding a presentable man, and she intended me for
this role. I was the acting fiancé, the son-in-law *in spe* and, as such,
I was duty bound to stick to family rules, one of which stipulated
that you weren't allowed to simply walk out of the festivities on a

special day like this, the *pater familias*' milestone birthday, or else it would skew the portrait—the family portrait in which the fiancé had his allotted place. Later on, when Mila brought home Sybille, the first woman she lived with, that wouldn't have mattered any more, let alone when she dragged in Adi. That evening, however, in spite of all the contemporary emancipation chitchat that Mila had absorbed but not digested, she still lived in fear . . . fear of her father, her mother and of what her parents' business associates and friends would say.

Mila put Pat down (or was it Fran she was holding?), patted Christine on the shoulder and came across the garden towards me.

'So?' she said. 'Take some good pictures?'

The hum of voices was audible through the open porch door before being drowned out by the stentorian tones of her father starting his speech.

'Come on,' Mila said, pulling me inside.

Incidentally, I did find her name, that is: ours. There was someone called Karst in the phonebook—just the surname, no address, which is why I had pushed a coin into the slot and dialled the number with shaking fingers. But no one answered. I'd written down the number, and when the speech was over—or rather speeches, for Mila's father's business partner had taken the floor after him, and then someone who had been introduced to me as the chairman of the local chamber of commerce—I had gone upstairs to the first-floor landing where there was a phone and had dialled the number again, and this time someone had picked up. A woman answered, not giving her name but saying 'Hello', as I did.

'Hello?' she said.

'Frau Karst?'

This was followed by a silence, a long silence during which I could hear my heart racing and pounding in my throat. But it wasn't her. Herr Karst had gone out. Now I realized it wasn't her. Her voice was completely different.

18

After moving away from Tautenburg, I had a dream I remember every bit as clearly as the two that came back to me later.

On a journey that took me through some remote parts of the country, I stopped in a village, parked the car and walked through the streets, and suddenly I noticed two elderly women glancing anxiously at me, and that's when I realized that they were hiding something from me. I walked up to them and pointed to a nearby house. So that, I said, is where she lived. At this, they looked at each other (their expression seemed to say: There's no point in lying) and nodded. Is that the house? I asked again. Every one of their movements betrayed their guilty conscience, and I thought that my mother must have run a very harsh regime. What other reason could there be for their lingering fear? Or did they believe I had come to continue her rule? I shone a torch into the rooms. All right, I said, now show me the grave. Was she buried under her real name? Yes, they said. So you knew her secret? Yes, but they were banned from telling me where she lived. They weren't allowed to ring or write to me.

This dream, which I had shortly after moving to Berlin, showed her in a different light than in my memory: as a despot whose attendants (for that was what they were) continued to fear her beyond the grave, whereas I mainly remembered the woman at the window, the shop window I passed on my way to school.

It had been years since I'd dreamt of her. I now presume that the dream was prompted by a card she had sent to Tautenburg and that Georg enclosed in one of his letters without any comment.

She always wrote the cards to me alone, and there was barely ever anything on them apart from: *Dear Philipp, I'm well. How are you?* The cards arrived irregularly, and since they never contained any mention of her address or the sender, you could only deduce her whereabouts from the postmark. Or since the two didn't necessarily match, not even that much.

Her initial motivation must have been to conceal her address from him, but she must have had another reason later, unless secretiveness was simply part of her character. She stuck to this habit of omitting her address even when I no longer lived with him in the slate town but somewhere else, and she no longer had to worry that the card would betray her whereabouts to him. Did she believe I might suddenly turn up on her doorstep or delve into her living circumstances against her wishes?

Yes, nothing but cards.

Cards with pictures of motorbikes or cars at first. Later on, art postcards: Cézanne's *Boy in a Red Waistcoat*, Magritte's *Empire of Light*, Caspar David Friedrich's *Woman at a Window*. Those are the cards I remember.

I kept them in the assumption that I could learn something about her from the choice of themes. I regarded them as a sort of secret message that it was my duty to decipher, and put them in a large envelope. I occasionally took it out to look at the pictures, and at some stage I realized that it had gone missing, or in any case I couldn't find it. None of the cards showed a cityscape, or if they did, for example in the case of the Rome card, then the view and the postmark didn't match up. It was a picture of the Spanish

Steps, but the card had been posted in a completely different city—Copenhagen.

But how did she know my address?

Three cities—Frankfurt, Berlin, Hamburg and then Frankfurt again—and often I had moved several times within those cities, and yet each time she very soon found out my address. How? Who was she in touch with? For a time, I suspected Georg. Perhaps he was only pretending not to know where she was. That wasn't possible, though. I could rule him out. Who else? Schwepp, I thought, Georg's friend. He must have been the one feeding her information about me. Yes, there was no other explanation. And she'd got the photos from him too. The same envelope in which I later found the passport photos contained pictures of me too, taken on the same day for many years—Georg's birthday. You could tell from the gathering, and the only one who had always been there and taken photos was Schwepp. He had always managed to arrange things so I was alone in the shot, occasionally with another guest but never with Georg.

It was a very large grey envelope on a pile of sewing patterns on the floor. The management of the home had transferred Herta's belongings to a windowless storeroom, lit only by a flickering neon light, so they could renovate her now-unoccupied room. I was about to toss the envelope into the paper-recycling bin when Mila, who was helping me clear out her things, stopped me.

'Don't,' she cried, taking the envelope from me and turning it over, and out fell the pictures Schwepp had taken along with the passport photo Herta had sent me, or rather the strip from which she had cut off two pictures, still joined together—yes, the same light, same haircut, same slightly forbidding expression. What about the fourth? Maybe she had used it for an identity card. Why else would you take this kind of picture?

The last time I met Schwepp was at his wife's funeral. Georg picked me up at the station and drove me to Siegen, where the Schwepps lived. He didn't take the newly built motorway but the country road we used to take via Kalteiche. Schwepp had had an operation on his nose the previous year. You could still see where the flaps of skin had been sewn together just above the bridge of his nose—a jagged line with different-coloured skin on either side. Now an old man, he moved with a certain frail dignity.

In my memories he is someone who would laugh at any opportunity, and he even appeared to be laughing on this of all days, a day of mourning that left him helpless and childish—until, that is, I noticed that this impression was due to the scar on his face. Whether he wanted them to or not, the corners of his mouth pointed upwards, and his crow's feet radiated out in odd contradiction to the horrified, indeed panicked expression in his eyes. They seemed to be laughing, whereas his eyes lay vacant and dull in their sockets.

So it was Schwepp. But he denied it when I asked him.

Years and years of cards, and then suddenly, many years after her death—so many I'd stopped counting—another letter.

I recognized her handwriting immediately; unlike his, it was irregular and fluttery, the letters slanting in all directions. If you held up his letters, with their clear, tidy writing, alongside hers, you would believe him to be a man of swift and lucid decisions, someone who knew precisely what he wanted, and think her uncertain and malleable—but the exact reverse was true. Although he was no less intransigent than she, he was more cautious, tentative and, even if he tried to fend it off it, more buffeted by chance. Everything demonstrated as much: his journey to Hanover, his manner in Bonn, his attempts to sell the camera.

Dear Philipp, she wrote. *I shall move back to Tautenburg on 27 July and buy a house at least as big as your grandparents' in Plothow, with seven rooms in which you will always be a welcome guest. My only request is that you pick me up from the station.*

Then her precise arrival time: 21.18.

This letter announcing her return, which arrived shortly before the 27th, contained no more details about the sender than the cards had, but it was clear from the postmark that it had been mailed from Mittenwald, not far from the castle hotel where she, as someone reported to me many years later, apparently worked as a housekeeper.

That evening I drove to Tautenburg and walked into the station, where I saw from the timetable that she must have got her times mixed up. There was no train that arrived at 21.18. The next train she could arrive on came in shortly after half past ten, and the last one at a minute to midnight.

Fearing that she might have taken an earlier train, I had a look in the cafe on the other side of the square. *Maybe she's waiting there*, I thought, but I couldn't spot her anywhere, so I left again and sat down on the station steps. It was still light, with darkness settling slowly over the town. The tower loomed like a raised finger on its hill. Now and again, a car full of young people cruised past with the windows down and the radio turned up loud so that the thumping bass reverberated around the square. The occasional car pulled up by the steps and then sped off with a squeal of tyres without anyone getting out. When the train was announced, I got up, walked through the underpass and went up into the station.

Yet she was sitting neither in that train nor in the next, which arrived at one minute to midnight. I waited until everyone had got off. A girl dragging a duffel bag behind her and an old man who disappeared into the underpass without looking round: they were the only passengers to disembark. Unsure what to do, I stood around for a while, then walked to my car and drove back to Frankfurt.

A month later, a second letter arrived in which she wrote that she had looked out for me in vain at the station.

This letter had no sender's address either and since, as in the first, she made no mention of where she was, it was once more the postmark alone that provided some information. It was smudged, almost illegible, but after studying it through a magnifying glass, I thought it might say Tautenburg.

Of course, I thought, what else? When she wrote that she had looked out for me at the station, she meant she had gone back to Tautenburg. But, I thought next, it didn't necessarily mean that. If she had got the arrival date as wrong as she had the arrival time—that is, if she had come the day before or the day after and seen no one standing on the platform waiting for her—then it was possible she had continued her journey.

'Philipp,' Mila said when I told her about it later on the phone. 'Philipp, that's impossible.'

A few days later, I went to Tautenburg again. This time I took the train. It was early September and school had started again. Children were walking through the streets in orange caps with huge satchels on their backs; peering anxiously left and right, they waited at the lights and charged across as soon as it went green. After crossing the stream, I went through the stone arch that marked the beginning of the old town. This was the route that tourists who had ended up here by accident took—main street,

street to the castle—I stopped outside the shop where she had once worked, looked through the window and saw her there, in the same shop. There had been several changes of ownership and the old name had lost its lustre, but it still sold clothing and fabrics.

She was just bending down and as she stood up again, I looked her right in the eye. Separated only by a pane of glass, we stared at each other, I at her and she at me, and without showing the slightest surprise, she gave a signal I immediately understood. She raised one hand and wagged her index finger the tiniest amount— the warning she used to give me when I stopped by the shop window after school to wait until she came out; the same gesture and, as before, I took a step back and automatically looked around to check he hadn't suddenly appeared. Georg. After all, it was late morning, the time of day when he usually did his shopping. I hadn't mentioned her letters to him nor that I'd be coming to Tautenburg, and so I slunk into the shadow of the building in the hope that he wouldn't see me if he really were to come past. After a while, though, I walked over to the bench surrounded by flower tubs in the pedestrian zone and sat down.

The last time I had seen her was six years earlier. She knew I'd wanted to move to Frankfurt and had looked me up in a phonebook on her way through, found my number and called me. That was how she arranged meetings. That was what she had done in Berlin, where she had rung up several times on her way through, and she did so that time in Frankfurt.

It must have been winter, yes a day of record low temperatures. The radio in the darkroom was on, and it gave constant warnings of black ice. The cold front was moving southwards like a steamroller, and they kept interrupting the schedule for a fresh alert. Now, the radio said, the cold front has reached Göttingen, now Kassel, now Marburg, followed by a warning to drivers. The phone rang just as I was examining some photos in the water bath. I turned the radio down, picked up the receiver and heard her voice.

She was sitting, as agreed, in the restaurant above the station concourse with a cup of coffee. She got up as I walked in and sketched a hug by pulling me against her shoulder.

'So,' she said after I'd sat down. 'So?'

And then something I couldn't explain began. Silence as she scanned me with her eyes. She was in her late fifties at the time, but she looked younger. As always, her hair—which she probably dyed because there wasn't a single grey hair to be seen—was loose. No change in her style of dress either: she always wore soft, flowing dresses or suits, always in unremarkable colours. She observed me, and I observed her; and after a while she called the waiter over, paid and stood up.

It was about half past nine when we went down the stairs to the station concourse. At the bottom, she sketched another hug and, unlike in Berlin where I had sometimes resisted this leave taking and followed her, I turned immediately for the exit before glancing round again after all.

She had no luggage other than her handbag, which is why I presumed that she had gone to the lockers, and that is precisely where I saw her. She was not alone but in the company of a man who had hooked one arm under hers, a light-brown suitcase in his other hand. They were coming straight towards me, and so I stepped behind a newsstand and watched them head slowly to the platforms.

That was the last time I had seen her, six or seven years ago.

173

After a few minutes she came out. A thin cardigan was hanging over her shoulder and the dress she was wearing left her still-slender and slightly suntanned arms bare, but for the first time I noticed the scattered light patches from her wrists upwards. As before, her hair was loose and her style of dress was still the same, but her gait, once so spry, appeared more hesitant now, as if she were worried about falling over. She sat down beside me and put her hand on my knee.

'How lovely,' she said. 'How lovely that you came!'

This conversation (if it was one) took place many years ago and so I can't remember how it unfolded, not even if we had one or, as before, simply sat there in silence, but I do know that I stayed overnight in Tautenburg and wondered whether to call him before dropping the idea; I could have stayed with him, of course, but I chose to go to a hotel. And I know something else too: I noted down her address. *Fabritiusstrasse 17*, it says in the notebook I was using at the time and have found again.

Her house was very different to the one she had lived in before she disappeared, and yet there was something provisional about this room as well. That's right: just a room again, a single one, furnished again, and again dominated by the compact sewing machine she'd set up on the dining table. I saw it when I gained entry that afternoon.

When she had walked back into the shop with the same rueful shrug as ever, I went to the hotel on Bismarckplatz, filled out the registration form and went back out into the open air, which radiated a late-summer warmth in the early afternoon, then walked past the old council buildings and the stud farm and, at the end of Solmsstrasse, turned into Mittelfeld, which forked off into Fabritiusstrasse. It was one of the buildings from the fifties, with a small wooden porch to keep the wind out. There were two names alongside the doorbells, but hers wasn't one of them, and as I was considering what to do, the door opened and a woman appeared, pulling a pram behind her.

'Are you looking for someone?'

'Frau Karst,' I said without thinking.

'Frau Karst?'

'Yes, I'm her son.'

At this, the woman turned around and called into the house, 'Mum, Frau Karst's son's here.'

At this, a second door behind the door opened, the door to the ground-floor flat, and an old woman stuck her head out.

'She isn't here,' she said.

'I know.'

'Well, come on in.'

The young woman pushed the pram out through the front garden, and the old woman led me up the stairs.

'I'll open up so you can wait inside,' she said.

And that is how I managed to sit for half an hour, at least, in her room and look around. The time hadn't yet arrived when you carried your whole office around with you in your mobile phone, along with a built-in camera as standard, but I almost always had a camera with me, not one of the large ones I needed for my work but a small one I used to assist my memory. That day, however, all I had was my notebook. I took it out after a while, opened it and then put it away again without having written anything, which is why only a few details stuck in my mind and were also fixtures of her room at the home later: the sewing machine, of course, the glass lamp, and the countless ashtrays. Or were they, like the fabrics, still in one of the two suitcases standing by the window and only appeared after her accident, as she called the event that had prompted her move to the home?

The house was halfway up the hill and her room was on the first floor at the front, which meant you got a view of the town from here, and although you couldn't see the slope on the other side of the river, you could see over the roofs to the bell tower of the Catholic church, the enamel factory and the stud farm's stables and riding arenas from which there came the sound of neighing and scraping hooves.

19

I now visited her more often. Visits? No, they couldn't really be called that, not yet. I drove to Tautenburg and waited outside the shop that used to be Herzog's and was now called something with 'Market' in its title—one of those ten-a-penny names. I'd wait on the corner and when I caught sight of her coming out, I would follow her at a slight distance so that, should she look round, she wouldn't immediately spot me. She always took the same route, from home to shop and from shop to home.

Home? She only had that one room, and was in her late 50s. Such a small world—how was it possible? It's fine at 20, or even 30. Or after a tragic event, a breakup for example or a death, when the numbness caused by the pain blocked out the makeshift arrangements until you awoke from your apathy, gazed around and began to order your life anew.

But what was up with her? She walked along Solmsstrasse, taking big strides, heels clattering, bag dangling from her shoulder and a little bracelet sparkling on her wrist. Two women of her age came out of one of the streetside doors of the chancellery, clad in suits and hairstyles like silvery-blue helmets. They walked along in front of her for a while so I could watch all three of them until the two other women crossed the street, approached a car and unlocked it, and now I thought she began to walk more slowly and stare at them.

What was she thinking? Was she making comparisons? Was she contemplating how the two of them, having concluded their transactions in town, would now return home to their family and their community, while only her room awaited her?

But then I thought that maybe I'd got it all wrong; maybe she'd had all of those things, not here but in the town where she lived before her return. Maybe she had led a completely different life there, with a husband, friends and a big group of friends from whom she was enjoying a few weeks off to put in an appearance here.

And all of a sudden, as I saw her walking past the stud farm, past the flowering tubs in the entrance, I thought that her return must be a prank, another act in her game of hide-and-seek, maybe the last and most sophisticated of all which, like her cards, phone calls and stations rendezvous she had summoned me to, served one purpose and one purpose only—to fool us as to her real circumstances. Us? Me and him. She wanted to prove to us that nothing had changed, that she was the same person, still the same woman as the one who had gone away, and sear her image into our brains before disappearing for ever.

I crossed the bridge and as I looked up, it was the same dark town, this cramped, slate-grey, stifling town, and suddenly the hatred was back, like an old friend—the hatred I only felt so pointedly here, in the town I knew better than any other, which is why I felt so balefully bound to it. It was, without doubt, the hatred the child had felt, the adolescent who heard a slip of the tongue in every word. None of it had changed—the Obertor bridge, the yard of the textile factory, the gazebo overlooking the stream, the old town hall, the pub by the fountain I entered through a low gate. A steep flight of stairs led up to the first floor, but all there was on the ground floor was a long bar, curved like a question mark, which took up virtually the entire room, and the only seat other than the bar stools was a bench with russet-coloured leather cushions by the window. Here it was: Greiner's world. There they sat: the heirs to a fortune accrued over generations and often squandered in a single generation—here, the house of a late childless aunt; there, the grandfather's meadow; here, a field become a building plot—the red gourmet-mushroom faces, the chummy conviviality, the land-lord's slick at-your-service face with the apron tied behind his back, the brass sparkle of the counter, the beer taps and the lamps, this whole disgusting, staid, clubby ambiance, reeking of saddle leather and golf clubs . . . I drained my glass in one swig and was out in the street again in a flash.

I phoned Mila from the station, but she wasn't there; in any case, she didn't pick up. I stood in the phone box, staring out at the deserted square, and all at once I thought of the story she had told me about the painter she had visited in Italy.

She had known him for years. Only moderately successful at first, he had led a relatively frugal life as he looked for an affordable studio. He came into some money around about the time Mila gave up her job at the theatre and moved to Berlin. A few articles about him, published in quick succession, caused the prices to rocket of the pictures he kept painting over to save space and materials.

A couple of years later, Mila received a letter from him inviting her to visit him in Italy. We had already split up but had decided to travel to Abruzzo together, and it would be easy to combine the two. She took the train from Rome to Rieti, while I went to Palestrina and took the bus into the mountains from there.

'You can come along,' she said, but I didn't feel like it, and so we agreed that she would meet up with me a few days later. However, a week passed and she didn't show. The bedroom of the house I had rented had a view of the petrol station where the buses stopped, and when she still hadn't arrived after eight or nine days, I thought she had swapped me for him. So to escape the juddering loneliness of the prison the house had become, I went down to the petrol station, rented a car and drove into the mountains to Subiaco and on to L'Aquila.

We were already separated and she had discovered her preference for women, and yet I noticed how jealousy was consuming me. As if to avenge myself for her cheating on me, I spent the evening scouring the bars for an attractive woman but found none it would have been fun to spend the night with (as a way of creating a stalemate). Or rather: I recoiled from the idea of waking up alongside a stranger the next morning.

Getting back from Bellegra the following day, I noticed that the windows I had closed before leaving were open. Mila was sitting on the wall outside the house, smoking; and, too tired to argue, I listened to her account.

The painter (whose name was Heinrich but after purchasing the Italian house he had started to call himself Enrico) had picked her up from the railway station, driven her into the mountains and assigned her two rooms with a communicating door and a small lake outside.

He couldn't deal with all his land on his own and so, three times a week, a gardener would come and walk around with a poison-sprayer strapped to his back. When Mila went to her window in the mornings, she saw this man, enveloped in a white cloud, striding through the vineyards that came right up to one side of the house; Enrico was following him at a safe distance. As soon as he caught sight of her, he would wave, return to the house, shower and get changed.

Behind the house the previous owner had built a tennis court that Enrico had pointed out to her as soon as they arrived. He was as bad at tennis as she was and yet he persuaded her to try it out, and so they faced off in the midday sun and thrashed balls into the net or into the high wire meshing that surrounded the court like a cage.

Lunch was prepared by a girl who cycled up from the village and served the dishes out on the terrace. In the evening he drove Mila to a restaurant perching like an eagle's nest on a rocky crag, beckoned to the waiter, asked what he would recommend, and when they got home, he placed a bottle on the table and enquired whether she fancied sitting on the terrace with him for a while.

When she said, after a few days, that she had to leave the next morning, he replied, visibly shaken, that her plan was totally out of the question because he first had to show her the farmers' market in Rieti, and since the market was only held once a week and she could see how much it meant to him, she gave in and another few days passed.

They had never really been friends, nor did he make any passes at her, so she wondered what his reasons might be for showering her with such attentions. She had visited his studio once when he was still unknown and written an article about him. Was she supposed to do the same again now that his circumstances were so changed? Was he keen to correct his portrait from back then? He didn't need her to do that, though. In the very days before her departure, she had seen a report in a Sunday supplement with photographs of him on the self-same terrace on which they sat at night.

And now, inadvertently at first, she began to observe him and how he spoke to the gardener, the girl and the waiter. She noticed that he was always around her, within sight so to speak, even when he was talking to someone else. When he went into his studio, he left the door open so she could see him mixing paints. When she sat out on the terrace with a book around midday, she would see him at a slight distance, tying up a bush or mending a bike. If she went upstairs for a siesta, she heard him walking around the house, whistling, and if she came back down to carry on reading, he would emerge from his room, lie in the hammock and start reading too. It became clear to her that he had summoned her as a witness.

Yes, that was what it was. He needed her as a witness. It was not about her or anyone else writing about the house, the lake or the tennis court, but about his being seen. Just as other people told stories in words, he told stories merely by his presence, and when she left, there was no one left to listen to this wordless storytelling. It was the kind of storytelling at which the beggars you meet in major shopping thoroughfares in big cities were also accomplished: the legless man on the cart holding up a role of Band-Aid; the man with the cat who turned up every morning, as punctual as any employee, spread out his blanket in front of the bank, put the cat on his shoulder and stared meekly at the ground. They were all accomplished performers. They showed themselves off to passers-by, they put themselves on display, their bodies, their suffering and their poverty were the language with which they communicated, and that is exactly what her host did, the difference being that it wasn't his unhappiness he displayed to Mila—it was his happiness.

And, I thought as I travelled back to Frankfurt the next morning, Herta was no different. She had come to show herself off to us.

The shop in the street to the castle, her job, her shabby room, her lonely to and fro: these were her identity. And although I followed her and tried to find out about her life, now that I realized that this was her actual purpose, I was the one who felt observed by her. For years she had paraded her absence before me, and now she paraded her presence before me, and when she was sure she had managed to sear her image into my brain, she would vanish again, as suddenly as she had appeared, away from her makeshift arrangements in the slate town and back to her other life.

'No,' Mila said when I phoned her that evening and put my theory to her. 'That's absurd.'

I insisted it was true, though, and did not go to Tautenburg again until the business with the hat. Was it that autumn too? No, in the spring. Herta stayed there longer than I had anticipated and before Christmas she switched (as I found out only when it had already happened) from the still large but no longer exclusive clothes shop to the traditionally small menswear shop owned by Herr Kröger, an elderly man whose store was at the top end of the main street and who, amid general incomprehension as to how he managed to survive, had been selling gloves, shirts, ties, cufflinks, socks, scarves and hats for 40 years.

I learnt about this during an early-evening phone call. I had just got back from shopping and was standing in the kitchen unpacking bread, milk, fruit, the usual stuff, when the phone rang. I went out into the corridor and picked up. It was Georg.

'She's been taken to a home,' he said.

'Who?'

'Your mother.'

Then I heard what had happened. There had been just the two of them, Kröger and she, in the shop. At noon he went off to his regular restaurant where he had eaten his lunch every day for 40 years and when he got back he noticed a cluster of onlookers outside the shop window. He pushed his way through the crowd and saw her. Herta. She was sitting among the shirts, the gloves and the socks laid out in the shop window with a pair of scissors in her hand, and she was cutting the brims off the hats.

20

It was so unusual for Georg to ring me to give me news about Herta that for a while I succumbed to the illusion that there had been a change in his behaviour that would produce a change in her behaviour—a cautious rapprochement that would allow them both to pay attention to each other again. I thought it was possible that her breakdown—from which she recovered with amazing speed so that after some time she seemed no different from the person she had been before it—would usher in a new phase when they would get on with each other as normally as separated couples did. This was a misconception, however. Whenever I tried to tell her something about him, she would fall into a kind of torpor from which she would stir only when I changed the subject. She never gave any indication that she understood the content of my words or even the sound of them.

And he did the same.

In the weeks after her referral to the home, I went to Tautenburg more often than ever before or afterwards. The first thing I did was go to see him and report anything that had caught my eye during the last visit I'd paid her. She twisted her ankle, I told him once. Or if I went to see her afterwards: He's considering replacing the awning. Trivial things, everyday matters, but precisely for that very reason, I thought, better able to bridge the silence between them than any appeals to their reason would have been. It was as if I was probing for the chink through which my words might pass, but their armour was so impenetrable that they simply glanced off.

I usually went by train and took a taxi from the station because I didn't feel like waiting for the bus. He knew the arrival times and so he would wait in the kitchen, which was on the street side, as soon as he heard the car. Often, he would lead me around the house into the garden with its carefully tended lawn at the back of which redcurrant and gooseberry bushes bordered a vegetable patch with rows of beans and beds of onions, lettuces, carrots and strawberries.

He showed me what changes he had made and what he had recently planted and, turning around, we saw the pergola—a series of wooden arches over the path from the house to the shed that, much to his irritation, never became a real pergola. He had successively experimented with rambler roses, wisteria and clematis, but they refused to accept his invitation. They grew into bushes, which he tied to the posts with green plastic twine, but instead of climbing, they would bend away from them.

'Look,' he said, lifting up a tendril. 'Like this!' He would hold it up against the post to show me how the plant should have grown.

For a long time we had been the same height, but suddenly, as he stood up straight again, I noticed that he had shrunk. I could see over his head and I bent my hips slightly as if to hide our height difference from him.

After a while we walked up the slope into the house. He heated up the meal Frau Roth had prepared for him and then we sat down in the kitchen to eat. He had laid the table beforehand, setting out plates and glasses and placing the cutlery on napkins he had folded into triangles.

He asked four or five questions at once while he was still fiddling around at the stove. What are you working on? Have you got an exhibition? Is there a new book? Where are you going this summer? But he waved me away when I tried to answer. It was as if the few bits of news I had brought with me were too precious to be told in passing.

'Wait,' he said. 'Tell me after I sit down, all right?'

Yet as soon as he sat down, our conversation faltered and after a time I noticed that we had fallen so silent that suddenly there was nothing but the clatter of our forks on the plates.

He had worked out the questions before I arrived, and now I had answered them as briefly as he would have—the rule was always to play things down, treat them as trivial: a broken bone as a sprain, pneumonia like a cold—he no longer knew how to continue and nor did I, and so even before the end of the meal there was that familiar self-consciousness between us that could only be dispelled by getting up and turning to something else, something practical and visible, away from things contained entirely in words.

If I try to identify a pattern in our conversations, it would be the question-and-answer games I played as a kid.

Sometime after Herta had left, he gave me a book called *Ask Me: I Have 3,300 Answers*. The questions were on the left, the answers on the right. What is the capital of Bolivia? La Paz. What did the Sirens do? They lured fishermen to their deaths. I took the book everywhere to begin with, to school, to the swimming pool. When the other children came down to the fountain in the afternoons or to the yard later, I would pull it out of my bag and bombard them with questions. Which planet has a ring of meteorlike bodies? Who was the first man to fly over the South Pole?

What is a gumshoe? If the other boy knew the answer, I would hand him the book and it would be his turn to ask the questions.

It was an interrogation on the basis of knowledge that we had learnt by heart and had at our fingertips, and that was the pattern our conversations followed.

He: Where are you going this summer?

Me: Don't you want to pay someone to mow your lawn?

I answered with the name of a place, he with yes or no, and we would nod and move on to the next subject as if all there was to say had been said.

All our conversations remained superficial, but I don't think that was due to a lack of interest but something else, a drill we had rehearsed, a habit into which we unwittingly relapsed, a kind of timidity or deference. Or might I be wrong? Was this silence or inability to speak a characteristic of his before his breakup with Herta, one he had passed on to me? Maybe it wasn't the silence that was the problem but the assumption that it had to be broken?

After the meal, which had to be eaten because that was part of the whole visiting ritual, he felt the urge to go back outside. It was as if he was ill at ease in a kitchen and a house that had been configured entirely in keeping with his expectations and whose prevailing sense of order fitted him like a glove, and so his eyes began to wander helplessly. I observed this same thing on other occasions too, which is why I believe that his unease related less to the place than to the situation, being forced to sit opposite someone—and in this sense I was just another someone.

It was almost impossible to go into a cafe, as we once had, and simply sit there and wait until we had ordered and what we had ordered had been brought. He quite clearly experienced the inactivity to which he was condemned for those few minutes as a torment. After a while his impatience would turn to panic, a hounded look would enter his eyes, his hands would rummage in his pockets as if they were no longer part of him and were searching for something they couldn't locate, and it was not uncommon for him to drag me back out into the street before the waiter came and take a few swift steps and deep breaths.

The cafe was a trap, and the kitchen too had become a trap after lunch. Since he couldn't admit this (or didn't even realize it), I had to release him from it. It was my job to say: Let's go and sit outside. The furniture, the wallpaper, the carpets, the lamps, the pictures and everything else seemed to starve him of air, and so once he had put the dishes in the sink (I wasn't allowed to help), we would go back outside and sit on a bench pulled back under the protruding roof, even when it was late autumn or winter and really too cold for it. The sounds of the town drifted up to us, but the town itself was hidden by the fir trees at the end of the garden. They shielded the garden from the town like a shaggy black wall.

'Should I fetch you a blanket?' he asked.

'Don't worry,' I said, taking a few paces and sitting down again.

I stayed until late afternoon, pushed back my sleeve and glanced at my watch, upon which he got up without a word, went down into the cellar and came back up with two jars of Frau Roth's homemade jam. He put them in a plastic bag he had ready and pressed it into my hand.

Before Herta returned, if I had come by train he would say, 'I'll drive you to the station.' He didn't do that now. He knew I was going to see her and so he just saw me out. At the garden gate he gave me a tentative hug and, pulling away from me, a pat on the shoulder.

I walked along the street and if I looked back before the turn-off to the battery from where the town had been bombarded, I would see him standing at his fence with his hand raised. It was not a proper wave but a kind of signal that he was still there.

While she still lived in Fabritiusstrasse, I would follow the street the taxi had driven along, but later I took the path through the vineyard, the one frequented by lovers, went down a narrow flight of steps shortly before the station into the town and, after crossing the stream, walked uphill again past recent houses. They sat there, white in their freshly created gardens, pretending with their almost flat roofs and the ornate stained-wood balconies running all around the outside as if they were not here in this central German hill town but somewhere in the Bavarian Forest. Some imitated the farmhouses of Lower Saxony with brick facing, swooping roofs, and crossed wooden horses on their gables, and others looked like thatched island cottages; outside one stood a flag pole with a fabric fish hanging from it, fluttering in the wind. It looked like a collection of show homes, or as if a madman had got it into his head to greet Herta with the different building styles of all the regions where she had lived before she came back here.

In all, it was a 20-minute walk. The street zigzagged up the hill and once past the cemetery, you caught sight of the long building whose lower side wings and broad drive were, from a distance, more reminiscent of a hotel than a care home for the elderly. Only when you had passed through the gates and looked around did you realize that it wasn't that but something else—a last place. Old people with mobility problems stood in their playpens (advancing a few steps every now and then) on the earth path running around the lawn and flowerbeds, and on the lawn itself hunched human remains sat in their wheelchairs, which a kind nurse had pushed out into the sun.

She kept the curtains in her room drawn, apart from a small gap, and so the first thing you saw was the small lamp over the sewing machine, then her hands and her straight back, behind which a thin column of smoke rose from a cigarette lying forgotten in the ashtray.

Although she had lost contact years ago with the sales reps from whom she used to stock up with whatever she needed, she was always conjuring forth new bits of material and would sit there, bent over the machine with a needle between her pursed lips, staring at the length of fabric rattling away beneath her fingers. Her wardrobes were overflowing with dresses she had made for the kind of festivities to which she wasn't invited. Or no longer invited. She kept on sewing, though. It was as if she wanted to prove what a good idea it had been to purchase the sewing machine. *Self-imposed drudgery*, I thought, but she didn't see it that way.

It was a part of the ritual of my visits that she only noticed me some time after I had entered her room. Initially, I had stood near the door and cleared my throat in the hope she would look up, but later I would walk over without paying any attention to her sewing and place my hand on her shoulder. She would reach for it without turning round and raise it to her cheek. Eventually she would remove the needle from her lips and push it into her sleeve—always in the same spot, a hand's breath below her shoulder. She now had that brittle old woman's voice whose sound automatically reminded you of the mountains of cigarettes she had smoked over her lifetime and the lakes of gin fizz she had drained.

'Oh, let's go outside.'

Outside never meant properly outside in the garden with the playpens and the wheelchairs, but by the window. It wasn't that she wasn't allowed to leave the home, but she seemed to have lost all interest in doing so. She switched off the machine, stood up, opened the curtains and moved two chairs to by the window.

'Come on,' she said. 'Come on, Philipp, sit down.'

When I left, she would lead me along the corridors, past open doors through which you could see into the rooms, the bare interiors with beds to which her contemporaries' ancient frames were strapped, the self-harmers and the epileptics; and when I noticed the look she gave me out of the corner of her eye, that (disdainful?) searching look with which she registered my horror, I knew she didn't belong here. That she was only pretending to be confused. That she had faked the incident that she sometimes brought up in conversation as her accident or, if she hadn't faked it, she had recovered to the point where she could leave the home at any time but, for reasons unknown to me, preferred to stay.

Dragging the walk out to the extreme, she led me through that building echoing with voices and the clatter of rattling dinner trolleys before slipping her arm through mine when we came to the stairs.

'Careful,' she said, setting one foot gracefully in front of the other as we went down them.

She said goodbye by the door downstairs. She would bring me to the exit on the town side and stepping outside, I would see before me, on the other side of town, the slope, the White Rock, the Battery and, above the fir woods, the roof of his house.

21

December. An old assignment: to drive along and photograph the Romanesque Road for the magazine of a major newspaper. Castles, churches, the twin-towered cathedrals and basilicas, so to Quedlinburg, Halberstadt, Magdeburg, Jerichow and a final detour to Plothow. Back home on St Nicholas' Day, and the next day I got to work. I went down to the darkroom and developed the films I had in my case, first the ones for the assignment and then the ones from Plothow. I had photographed the old canal, the ice floes, the island lying under a blanket of snow, the park, the house, the street, all virtually unchanged; on the gable the remaining traces of the TV aerial Lilo's husband, Günter Mahrholz, and Georg had installed in the mid-fifties. I removed the pictures from the water bath and laid them on the drying table—yes, they were really good—went upstairs to the flat and when I came back down an hour later and looked at them again, I'd gone off them. They had a smoothness to them now; your eye slid off them.

Then, before Christmas, some mail from Lilo, a card showing the park in the snow, and an enclosed sheet of paper with a kind of letter thanking me for my visit. *Dear Philipp*—she uses my first name; anything else would sound false, of course, but, much as she insists, I have trouble reciprocating.

'What?' she said when I addressed her as Frau Mahrholz. 'Have you forgotten I'm your godmother?' And as I couldn't really call her godmother, she insisted that I call her by her first name. She no longer lived in Brandenburger Strasse but on one of the housing estates on the other side of the railway tracks: fifth floor, two rooms, kitchen, bathroom, a sweeping view of the town. She gave up the shop back in the seventies, and the house too; her sons—or, to be more precise, Günter's—tried to carry on running the store, but then they had got fed up with the hassle private businesses were subjected to and agreed to close down; one of them had taken a job at the washing-powder factory, the other lived in Magdeburg as a radio and TV technician.

And in February, the same week the magazine appeared, Frau Roth rang up and said, 'I don't know what your plans are for the house and maybe it's too soon to talk about it, but I know a young couple who'd be interested.'

The bungalow had been empty since Georg's death. With all the furniture still inside, it lay there in a kind of slumber from which it was awoken once a week when Frau Roth, who still took care of it, climbed up the hill to check that everything was all right. She would pull up the blinds, open the windows, let in some air and then close the windows again. In summer, when the grass had grown so long that it needed mowing, she would tell her husband and he would arrive with a small sit-on mower, and in winter she kept an eye on the heating which had to be on—albeit on the lowest setting—so the pipes didn't freeze.

When I went to Tautenburg a week later, she was waiting with the couple outside the house. Even though it was cold—there was even snow lying on the hill—she had refused to let them in. The man, who was in his early thirties with a buzz cut and a long black leather jacket offering a glimpse of a grey suit underneath, had taken over the local building society branch a few months earlier;

she had a hard, almost dried-out-looking girl's face and taught music and geography at the local secondary school. Both of them came from Tautenburg, as he stressed as if to underscore their moral rectitude. Having moved away after high school, they had now returned after a few years in the city.

Frau Roth unlocked the front door. I walked through the rooms, pulling up the blinds, then turned around and went out into the garden through the glass door. I felt a sudden reluctance to show these people around; Frau Roth ought to do it. As I trudged through the snow, making patterns, I saw them through the window moving from room to room, Frau Roth leading and the two of them following with an air of pre-emptive possessiveness. In the study, the hard-faced woman pulled a tape measure out of her bag, checked the distance between the door and the wall and then slung the tape measure around her neck, where it coiled up on the front of her black coat like a yellow snake. Eventually they went back into the corridor past the open glass door and stopped in the hallway.

That is when I heard him say, as if through a filter, as he pointed up at the trapdoor: 'Where does that lead? To the attic? May I?' And the next moment he was holding the wooden pole that was habitually propped up in the corner beside the door, pushing the hook on its tip into the metal ring; with a screech of springs, the trapdoor swung open and immediately afterwards came the grating noise of the ladder.

I went down to the fir trees, which rose up like a shaggy black, now snow-speckled wall in front of the fence and would be the first thing to fall when the place was sold, and rightly so; after all, the advantage of the house was its site and the view from up here. You could look out over the valley, or at least you could have done, had Georg not cut himself off from the town behind his fir wall.

'Herr Karst,' Frau Roth called as she stood halfway up the ladder behind the other two.

When I emerged into the attic, I saw the man standing under the dormer window in his long leather jacket. 'Do you know what happened here?'

He removed his hand from his pocket and pointed to something by his feet. The wooden floor was made of wide planks cut roughly to size and stippled with countless small black dots. Burn marks. Someone had stood at this window smoking, then dropped the butts and put out the embers with their shoe. I bent down, ran my fingers over the marks and shrugged my shoulders.

'No idea.'

When the couple had left, I climbed back up the ladder. There were three windows up there—small dormer windows set in the sloping roof, with rounded corners. One had a view of the hill that rose up higher behind the house, another south towards the Battery; both were rusted up and wouldn't shift when I tried to open them. Only the third one, from which one could look out over the town towards the slope on the far side, was easy to push open first time, and only under this one did the floorboards have scorch marks.

The home on the other side of town was in darkness, and only the top row of windows were lit. Running in front of them was a series of small balconies, one of which belonged to Herta's room. Just as he could see her window and balcony, she too had an unencumbered view of his house, well, of its roof; and with a powerful lens, a pair of binoculars, she would even have been able to see the dormer window where he was standing.

Yes, that's how it might have been.

Like wolves calling to each other across the town. How are you, my darling? Fine. How are you? How's your shoulder? Getting better. And your leg? Already healed.

Below them in the valley, the town, with the fairy-light glow of its streets, and the clustered lights of the station on its edge, at the end of an unsightly avenue, lined with fifties apartment blocks on one side and a chain-link fence on the other, with the railway tracks beyond it. At night, however, when the town lies in darkness, the station appears to be at its centre, to the half-hourly sound of rumbling trains, freight trains producing the deep frequency of dreams, the sluggish double stroke of steel wheels.

And the two of them up above, each on their hillside.

Her gaze is drawn to the slope on the other side of the town, which is divided into two virtually equal halves by the stream. Herta's eyes would seek out the marker of the black wall behind which, she knows, the roof of his house sticks up; it's hard to make out in the dark, whereas he only needs to look for the two long rows of lamps along the ends of the long building.

He stands by the open dormer window through which the earthy smell of the garden enters in the summer and the scent of snowy air in autumn, winter and spring; from November to April, it smells of snow up there. She leans forward in the small space between the curtain and her window, which is also open, only an inch though, enough to feel close to him. That way, all there is between them is air, which here near the cemetery smells of leaves and dead flowers. She doesn't want the night nurse to come in and see her here, so she has wedged the back of the chair under the door handle and turned off the lamp. Light filters up from the lanterns along the path, not much but still it disturbs her meditations, which is why she cups her hands to shield her eyes, whereas he simply stands there because there is nothing to distract his gaze up there. After the metallic screech of the trapdoor, all is still—only the sounds of night reach him, the trains, an occasional car, the wind in the firs.

They stand there for a while, listening. How are you, my darling? Fine. How are you? Then they turn away. He climbs down the ladder, and she steps back behind the curtain into the room and turns on the lamp on the chair by the bed, the lamp she brought back from her travels. It is made entirely of glass: the shade the colour of mother-of-pearl, the green tapering stand and the raspberry-red base, all of them made of shimmering matt glass.

They came to Tautenburg in April '57, she left the town again in January or February '58, and she came back in the summer of '87, 29 years later.

She had brought with her this glass lamp, the sewing machine and a number of ashtrays—receptacles in an enormous range of shapes and sizes made of china, glass, tin, cast iron or stamped metal, many bearing the name of the pub or the hotel they came from, and so it was possible to retrace her journey with the sole aid of these ashtrays. They used to stand around everywhere: on the table, the chest of drawers, the windowsill and the shelf over the washbasin—souvenirs among which she distributed her ash equally (as if none should be less favoured). She smoked, even though, all around the home, there were signs with a burning cigarette inside a red circle with a black line through it. She hardly ate anything but she smoked. When I visited her, I saw a little pile of ash in every container and so I automatically imagined her walking around with a cigarette in one hand.

The glass lamp, the ashtrays and the sewing machine, which I now believe she owned before she left Tautenburg: those were what she had brought back from her travels.

22

'That's a pity,' said Wüstenhagen when I dropped in on him. 'A pity you don't have the packaging. It looks brand new. It'd be nice if you still had the box, the original one.'

He turned the Varex this way and that, put it down on the table, then picked it up again, held it to his nose, sniffed it and shut his eyes. 'Amazing.' He kept it in his hand now; he obviously found it hard to part with. When he stood up, it lay there like a newborn baby in the crook of his arm and that's where it stayed as he walked through the shop alongside me. Cameras everywhere: old cameras, field cameras, plate cameras, folding cameras, an old Agfa Clack, a limited-run Voigtländer Dynamatic with a hot shoe to attach a flash, a Perkeo 3x4, folding rangefinder cameras with Skopar or Heliar lenses, vintage Hasselblads, the Leica developed by Barnack, the twin-lens Rolleiflex, a Kine Exakta, a Zeiss Contax, Polaroids, on shelves, behind glass, in display cabinets, all of them held to peoples' eyes times beyond counting, pointed at people beloved and hated, just met or soon to be left, at houses, gardens, rivers, bridges, beaches, theatres, museums, churches, schools, steps, stairs ascending and descending—and floating over it all, over the entire collection, a gentle, almost imperceptible aroma of oil, metal and leather.

The store and workshop are in Allerheiligenstrasse, next to the city drop-in centre. At your first glimpse of the shop window, a junk store that widens at the back, one room leading into the next until you enter the fifth or sixth and reach the centre, the inner sanctuary where Wüstenhagen, with a monocle in front of his eye, a tiny screwdriver in his hand, performs his repairs on the little marvels he considers cameras to be.

'So,' he said as we walked back the way we had come, 'how much do you want for it?'

'Don't know,' I said, stepping out into the street. 'I'll call you.'